SOPHIE'S THROUGHWAY

SOPHIE'S THROUGHWAY

JULES SMITH

Matador
9 Priory Business Park,
Wistow Road, Kibworth Beauchamp,
Leicestershire. LE8 0RX
Tel: 0116 279 2299
Email: books@troubador.co.uk
Web: www.troubador.co.uk/matador
Twitter: @matadorbooks

ISBN 978 1784623 852

British Library Cataloguing in Publication Data.
A catalogue record for this book is available from the British Library.

Printed and bound by CPI Group (UK) Ltd, Croydon, CR0 4YY

Typeset in 11pt Aldine401 BT Roman by Troubador Publishing Ltd, Leicester, UK

Matador is an imprint of Troubador Publishing Ltd

*This book is dedicated to the people who live outside
the box: the button pushers, the distinctive thinkers, and the
pioneers of new directions. To those who refuse to be labelled
as 'normal' and show those that live beside them how to
stretch their imagination.*

CHAPTER 1

"So you're saying I'm a retard?" Brendon challenged, his coat zipped right up to his bottom lip, arms folded and stinking of attitude.

"Brendon!" I scolded, "I've asked you repeatedly not to use that word. It's disparaging and inappropriate." As usual I reddened, embarrassed at his misuse of language and feeling inadequate as a parent.

"It's just a word," he replied, kicking a torn piece of paper on the floor in front of his muddy trainers, "everyone says it. Like they say someone's gay. Doesn't mean *they're gay* and gay is bad, it's just a word."

"Well it's the wrong word to use for all the reasons I've explained!" I shook my head at the silent doctor in front of us to reaffirm my disapproval.

"It's OK Brendon," said Kathy, the in house paediatrician. Actually, I didn't think it was OK but that wasn't what she was referring to. "Having Aspergers and PDA doesn't mean you have anything bad or seriously wrong with you. It doesn't mean you are stupid at all, you just see the world a little differently and may have trouble in social situations." She spoke calmly and maintained a relaxed demeanour unlike me; leant forward in my chair, arms crossed and pushing the balls of my feet into my shoes.

This was Brendon's first official diagnosis from a medical professional. For the last few years we had been through the inappropriate /unruly /rude /defiant and obnoxious personality descriptions from his teachers at school and pushed to do various tests from dyslexia to psychological profiling.

Although Brendon had been on a behavioural plan with the school Special Educational Needs team, they had called me in to say that he showed more than the *usual* ADHD traits and was definitely fitting the Aspergers profile. After thorough analysis it seemed they were right and here we were with a doctors diagnosis and a whole lot of bewilderment.

"Here's some information and some books to take home to help you understand autism better." Kathy handed the books over to Brendon who gave them a teenage look of disdain.

"I'll look it up myself, thanks." He stood to his feet and went to the door. "Come on," he urged, glaring out under his black fringe.

"Thank you very much." I smiled and took the books and leaflets from Kathy. That was it? A whole load of leaflets and a couple of books was all I was armed with?

Brendon didn't talk to me on the way back as I drove him to school. An uncomfortable silence filled the car. *How was he feeling about this?* It's one thing to know that your kid has social issues but to have an official label attached was something different. This was my child, my perfect child.

"Are you OK?" my words sliced through the silence like an accusation.

"Yeah…why wouldn't I be?" He remained looking forward, showing no physical emotion. But I was his Mum and I could feel it.

"We can go through this later, it's really nothing to be worrying about." He remained silent. I didn't push it as I knew well enough when to stop. Although I had no real understanding of Aspergers or PDA , I had learnt over time how to read Brendon and when it was wise to let him be. He got out of the car without a goodbye and I watched as he sloped through the school gates, trying to hold back my tears at his obvious pain. I went home and spent the rest of the day reading every leaflet and as many online reports on the subject that I could find.

ASPERGERS: *People with Asperger syndrome can find it harder to read the signals that most of us take for granted. This means they find it more difficult to communicate and interact with others which can lead to high levels of anxiety and confusion.*

Asperger syndrome is mostly a 'hidden disability'. This means that you can't tell that someone has the condition from their outward appearance. People with the condition have difficulties in three main areas. They are: social communication, social interaction and social imagination. Whilst it falls under the 'Autism' umbrella, people with Asperger syndrome have fewer problems with speaking and are often of above average intelligence. They do not usually have the accompanying learning disabilities associated with autism, but they may have specific learning difficulties.

Yes that made a lot of sense and seemed to fit Brendon quite well. I then moved onto PDA, something I'd never even heard of before. Apparently, some doctors married the two together and some saw them as quite different.

> PDA: Pathological Demand Avoidance: *People with PDA can be controlling and dominating, especially when they feel anxious and are not in charge. They can however be enigmatic and charming when they feel secure and in control. Many parents describe their PDA child as a 'Jekyll and Hyde'. It is important to recognise that these children have a hidden disability and often appear 'normal' to others.*
>
> *Many parents of children with PDA feel that they have been wrongly accused of poor parenting through lack of understanding about the condition. These parents will need a lot of support themselves, as their children can often present severe behavioural challenges.*

And that description fit him even better. I leant back in my office chair and sighed. In one of the collection of leaflets I'd been given there was a form to be completed by the parents, giving their account or experience to help both medical staff and teachers deal with his behaviour and set out strategies that would help him at school and at home. I decided to fill it in there and then whilst I was still in an emotional state; tell it how it is from a Mother's point of view; what it *really* feels like to have a son whom you love to bits and yet cannot seem to control no matter what you try to do.

I took a pen lying on my desk and began to write.

layman's terms from a Mothers experience:

Be prepared for strategic games at all times. If you can't play chess, learn it now as it will help. You have to be ten steps ahead and make them think that what you want them to do was their idea all along. This often doesn't work. Be prepared to be out manipulated and out smarted at every turn. Always be ready for inappropriate responses and behaviour; if your child thinks someone's got a big arse or he doesn't like them, he'll tell them. To others your child will seem like a cocky, obnoxious reprobate; sometimes you will think the same but you will also see the vulnerable person who can't cope with reality. Do not buy nice things for your house for they will only get trashed when he goes on a MELTDOWN. You will be shown an honest and somewhat refreshing individual who is full of wit and charm but you will also be taken swiftly from that euphoria and kicked into the detritus of despair. Know that you will be judged by those that are ignorant on the subject of autism and think you clearly have no concept of parenting. Have tools that enable you to cope in a crisis like: good red wine, comedies and excellent friends. And chocolate. Definitely chocolate.

CHAPTER 2

At age fifteen and a half, Brendon was that wonderful mix of Aspergers and raging puberty that made you want to run away to a remote cottage in Cornwall or commit mass homicide. As only a Mother of an Aspie kid knows, the world just doesn't give you enough credit for the amount of hell you have to endure.

His sister Bryony was fourteen years old, going on twenty and though *also* teeming with hormones, was on the whole, a well behaved kid. Their Dad was Karl. Karl Rhodes. Sorry, I should say "Rhodes, Karl Rhodes," because that's how he said it when anyone asked his name.

"Do you think you're James Bond or something?" I once asked as he delivered his moniker to a salesman.

"It helps people remember your name if you say it like that, Sophie."

Karl was a very enigmatic man and a social chameleon. He could hold an audience with people from all walks of life and fit right in. Everybody loved him instantly. It seemed to be more important that everyone else thought he was marvellous than actually adopting the same princely behaviour at home, and though he professed undying love and commitment, he did so like he was reading from a script.

Karl and I had children early on in our relationship, pretty soon after getting married. He *apparently* 'loved kids' or so he professed and couldn't wait to start a family whereas I was more than a little hesitant. Turned out I was the one who found the all giving, life committing bond with our offspring and he found it all too much of a hassle and interference. Of course, Brendon's behaviour hadn't helped. Aspergers had a way of altering that idealistic, perfect family of four set up. Holidays were always fraught and more comparable to an endurance test rather than a relaxing getaway and life at home, was at most times, demanding and chaotic. It was difficult to stay a strong united front but even more so when you had opposing ideas and methods on dealing with Aspergic defiance and thuggery. Karl didn't buy into modern day labels and believed that harsh lessons and Dickensian methods always put people in check. The relationship between Karl and Brendon was always a slight groan off volcanic eruption and it didn't help that Brendon thought his Dad was a dick.

"What have you ever done for me?" Go on… name it… NAME IT!" Brendon shouted at his Father one Saturday afternoon. "Did you teach me to ride my bike? No, that was Mum. Did you ever stop to listen to how I felt? No…'cos you *think* you know everything… Did you ever spend time playing with me? No, not really. You've basically done *fuck all* as a parent!"

"Who do you think you are, you silly little boy," Karl mocked, the Alpha male aggressor emerging, "I put food on the table, give you a house to live in and *you* are an abusive and cocky little shit!"

"Please don't say that," I whispered harshly at Karl, "you're the adult remember, that won't help." I'd read up on all the strategies of how to deal with defiance but seemed to be the only parent trying to put them in place.

Neither one of them listened to me as I pleaded for them to walk away from each other. Both were heightened with rage and an inbuilt desire to win no matter the consequence.

"You're a fucking dick, stay out of my way!" Brendon spat at his Dad. "Asshole."

Despite being English, Brendon tended to talk, shout and spell in American due to the amount of time he spent on his computer. He was an IT genius and the world wide web and gaming was his life. He had adopted the huge table downstairs as his own and it sat with 3 flat screen monitors and a state of the art, self built, computer on top. Computing and life behind a screen was his world and the only thing that could be used as a threat against unacceptable behaviour.

Karl marched through the room into my study, which was located next to Brendon's Starship Enterprise get-up, and ripped out the router instantly killing the internet. No internet equals no games. No games equals MELTDOWN.

"There ya go, smart arse!"

" Give me that back now or I'll break EVERY fucking

thing that you own!" Brendon's eyes were black and his breathing was rapid and shallow. It didn't take a genius to see he was about to flip out.

"Don't you threaten me! Touch anything of mine and I will take everything you own and dump it at the tip."

"Stop, please stop. STOP NOW!" I wailed, knowing it was futile but trying nonetheless.

Brendon flew at his Dad and pushed him hard in the chest. At 6'2" and 14 stone in weight, he was a big lad for his age and not easily controllable. Karl grabbed him in a head lock to stop him. They wrestled together around the room and crashed into my bookcase; my antique bookcase, full of lovely books, but what did they care? It teetered precariously on it's oak carved feet and the the glass doors flung open, spewing books onto the floor. The doors slammed shut as they bounced into it again causing one to shatter. Splinters of glass lay shiny and menacing on the carpet as though mocking their fractured relationship. I ran forward and tried to prize them apart, screaming and begging them to stop. Framed pictures depicting natures calm, bounced from the walls as they danced their way round the room, their wooden frames and fronts splitting all over the floor.

"MUM!" I heard a shout in the hall from Bryony.

I rushed into the hallway to see my frightened little girl, crying and trembling.

"Make them stop, it's scaring me."

"Put on your shoes and go outside to my car," I spoke calmly. " I'll be there in a minute."

I went back to the battlefront where the shouting and

cursing had increased. My room looked like it had been burgled. " WHY WON'T YOU STOP?" I pulled hard at Karl's t-shirt. "You're both scaring Bryony and me." Tears pricked my eyes and my breath wedged in my throat. My efforts were fruitless. Once enraged there was nothing I could do. I didn't have the physical strength to part them and my pleas were like whispers in a gale.

"MUM, TELL HIM TO GET THE FUCK OFF ME!"

"Karl let him go, let him go right now!" I pushed at his shoulder. The sound of my son begging for his Mother's help was a powerful call.

"I'll let him go when he stops coming at me, when *he* learns to be respectful and knows his goddam place." The words came out in a low growl as he pushed Brendon to the floor. I was at a loss and torn between helping my son, stopping a fight and rescuing my traumatised daughter outside in the car. I burst into tears of frustration and made the decision to leave. I went to my car, physically shaking and wiped my tears away with the sleeve of my jumper. I had to play this down in front of Bryony and look like I had at least *some* element of control.

I slipped into the drivers seat and reached over to hug her as she cried into my shoulder, her long, curly brown hair sticking to my jumper like ribbons of velcro.

"Why do they do this? Why won't Dad just walk away? I don't like it when they fight it really frightens me. It scares my friends when they come over."

"I know. It's stupid," I agreed rubbing her back, "don't

worry, it's part of what we have to deal with in this family. I will always look after you. They're just having a battle of control, it will sort itself out, it always does." I smiled faintly, trying to believe my own words.

"Let's go get an ice cream!" I suggested to her blotchy, tear stained face. I saw a glimmer of safety return to her grey eyes as I started the car. All the way to the shop I was praying to God and other mystical beings that Brendon and Karl wouldn't kill or harm each other. I was praying and wishing so hard, it hurt me to breathe.

CHAPTER 3

I spent the majority of the evening sat on the carpet amongst shards of glass and splinters of wood, holding my boy who was crying like his heart had broken. It was like handling a gigantic toddler after a major strop who was now beaten with raw emotion. He refused to let me leave his side, clinging on to me like I was his only safety net and blocking any form of exit. He didn't want to talk, just cry.

Every now and then, when earlier events played through his mind, he would violently thump the chair at the side of him with such force, his knuckles bled.

"I HATE him, I want him to leave." His words came out broken with the gruffness of strained vocal chords.

"Shhh." I whispered, "this has to stop. You have got to learn how to speak to people, particularly adults. You can't just go at people when you feel like it."

He pushed me away abruptly and began to sob violently into his hands. "Why are you on HIS side? What the fuck Mum?"

"I'm not on anyone's side. I don't agree with how either of you behaved." I pulled him back to my arms.

Of course, he was my main priority and the one I wanted to protect but if I voiced that he would see it as a green light to kick off whenever he felt like it. My job was to help him fit into the social norm so he could be accepted and not pushed away by others. He *had* to find a way because the world was not going to change for him.

"I want the router back. Get it from him. He shouldn't just take stuff away. He's a bad parent and I hate him."

"No, he's not. He loves you. I'll see what I can do about the router but no promises," I soothed. "Go to bed, get some rest."

"Get it back, I mean it." He lifted himself from the carpet, his t shirt ripped from the brawl and raised, angry scratch marks down his arm. I winced at the sight of my child in this state.

As he lumped himself upstairs I went into the lounge where Karl was sitting watching the news. His face was tight and his stare was way beyond the physical being of the newsreader represented on TV. He was in another place and I knew he found it unbearable. God knows I did.

"We need to talk about this." I sat on the edge of the sofa and clasped my hands in my lap waiting for him to reply.

"Not now, I'm really not in the mood."

"Neither am I but we can't go on like this. I can't have you both fighting like that, its horrendous. It scares me and it scares Bryony; she was in tears."

Silence.

"*Please*, you need to walk away from it and not react, I *know* it's hard but coming back at him just provokes the situation, not help it. You *are* the grown up remember."

"Right now I couldn't give a flying fuck about who the adult is," he spat. "He uses Aspergers as a fucking excuse and it's not. I want him out of this house. I cant live like this anymore. He goes or I do."

Clearly now wasn't the right time. Neither one of them appeared to be rid of their 'ego humungous'. But when was the right time?

"I get it. I know it's difficult not to react but what happened earlier isn't going to work. Your son hates you, he believes you hate him, he's got scratches on his arm…"

"Yeah where I was holding him by his shirt when he threw himself to the ground. I didn't hurt him Sophie, *is that what you think*? I just stopped him from pushing his weight around."

"Whatever. It's still not right," I continued, " and he wants the router back. You should have warned him before you just took it away. That's what we've been told to do. To give warnings. Three chances."

"I don't *care* what we've been told to do by these psycho babbling, hippy-fied, do-gooders who have *no* comprehension of what we live with everyday. That child needs to get a grip and learn to respect the rules of this house or get out."

He snatched the remote and killed the newsreader mid sentence. I waited like a berated child, wondering if he was still going to talk or not. He threw the TV control on the sofa and without even looking at me, said, "I'm going to bed," and left the room.

I felt depleted, angry and useless. I didn't cry very often but the sobs came involuntarily, like exorcised demons. I stayed, head in hands, until they finally abated.

***

On the day Karl left he stood on the threshold like a man torn in half. A man on the crossroads of choice; neither being a road he wished to travel down. Though tall and stocky he appeared as a weak and shattered resemblance of his former self. I didn't believe he would actually go but the fighting and the strain of our day to day life had triumphed over any shred of love that was left.

"I'll miss you and I'll always love you," he whispered. As his eyes looked up from his bent head, they were filled with tears.

I gripped the Victorian radiator in the hallway, hoping that the heat burning through the enamel into my hand would somehow deaden the sickening pain that was threatening to engulf my entire being.

"I know." I replied, "I know."

CHAPTER 4

Nearly six weeks had passed by since Karl's departure and though it was hard to maintain my job and a structured, non deviating, Aspergers friendly regime at home, I'd managed to make it so far. Brendon had become more tyrannical than ever insisting that he was now 'man of the house.' He played the role of despot a little too well and had taken to telling Bryony what she could and couldn't do.

I had found it difficult to sleep, what with the break up and the work load and my appearance was suffering. The heady days of waking up fresh faced and dewy eyed were a thing of the past: it was more like sallow skinned and bad hair day 24/7. I made the decision to have my long hair cut off into a short bob that just tucked neatly behind my ears and was easy to get done at 6.30 in the morning. I wasn't sure whether I had done this because it made life simpler or I was reinventing myself as a single woman, *trying* to be in charge of her life. The new look did not go down very well with Brendon. Aspergers and change do not walk down the same street.

"You look like a lesbian," he said blank faced as he

looked at me, " I hate it and I don't want to look at you." He walked off to his computer desk to avoid me.

"Really. That's nice." I shouted after him. "And exactly what do lesbians look like?"

"Like that." He turned and nodded in my direction without making eye contact.

"Well good for lesbians, for they are clearly the most beautiful and stylish women on the planet. I don't like the way you pigeon hole people Brendon, we have discussed this and it's wrong." I followed him through to his computer station.

"Whatever fam." He turned on his screens and began to load World Of Warcraft, League of Legends and Facebook simultaneously.

"How would you like it if someone said, 'You look autistic or you must be like Rain Man?"

"What? Who's Rain Man?"

"Never mind. The point is that you're not and you are an individual. That's how you should treat everyone." I pressed.

"Mother, I really don't care what people think of me, so can you please desist from nagging like a fishwife and leave me to my guild." He sat down, put on his noise reduction headphones and began to type and Skype to his warrior friends.

I left him to go and make dinner and hoped that every time I said these things they were actually sinking in.

"Your hair looks lovely," Bryony appeared in her 'Girl Power' onesy. She was beautiful. Frighteningly so. Although only fourteen she looked much older and stood at 5'7" with a figure that belonged in glossy magazines.

"Thank you, angel." I hugged her tight. I was mindful to give her as much attention as possible since Brendon demanded the majority of it. We cooked lasagne together and chatted about boys and homework and Justin Bieber. I was very careful to remain positive on this subject despite thinking he was a precious little diva.

I served the portions of lasagne and poured myself a well deserved glass of Rioja and spent the next three minutes removing every trace of mushroom from Brendon's food. He hated them passionately and if one was to be present on his plate, the whole dinner would have been ditched.

"Bren, your dinners ready," shouted Bryony as she set the table with knives and forks.

Brendon was a world away. A virtual, sword wielding, spell making world away.

"What the fuck are you doing man? You noob, Tom! Focus Katarina…I'm going in…have you got ult?…" he was shouting directions to his team members through his mic. I sighed and wandered through to his room and tapped him on the shoulder.

"DINNER."

He pulled his headphones to one side. "You'll have to bring it here I'm in an instance. Thanks Mommy, I love you, you're the best." He returned to his virtual world and I brought his dinner to the Starship Enterprise. Some things weren't worth an argument.

Once we had eaten Bryony scurried away to snapchat her friends whilst I slumped on the sofa with my iPad and some background TV. I clicked on the word game app on my tablet. I'd been playing an online scrabble game for a good year whenever I got a spare minute. I loved it and it kept me focussed and distracted from my reality. I had a few friends on there and some random players that I'd played with for some time. They were a nice bunch, mostly from the States since I tended to play in the evening or when I couldn't sleep at night. I only had about five games so I decided to get another opponent as the others didn't seem to be in speedy, play mode. I pressed random play and a new game appeared.

My opponent was called '*The Voice*'

S P T G E O D were my letters. Despot, I could play despot. How wildly appropriate.

SOPHISTICATED played Despot for 12 points.

My word appeared on the virtual board with a musical tring.

After one glass of wine and an hour of the History channel my body was giving up the will to function and the soft downs of my huge empty bed were beckoning. I got up and went to fetch a glass of water and noticed that Brendon was still playing online.

"Brendon, it's past 11, you should go to bed now it's school tomorrow." I stood at his side, repeatedly yawning.

"I'm not going - it's French and I hate French. The

only good thing about it is my teachers fit and has an awesome pair of... you know, she has a very pleasant personality Mother!" he finished with a wicked grin.

I heard the cackle of pubescent boys through the Skype channel at the thought of Miss Frenchy's upper assets.

"You're going," I insisted. "Besides, I'm coming in for your weekly review with Mrs. Armitage in the morning."

"Oh God, another wasted hour of my life."

"Bed." I left the room and made my way upstairs, desperate for sleep.

I slipped into the sheets and shivered. The huge, super-king sized bed was so cold with just me inside. I reached down to the floor and retrieved my hairdryer where it had been tossed after drying my lesbian haircut earlier. I turned it on underneath the sheets to warm them up until I got the temperature to a point where I knew I could maintain it with my own body heat and went to switch off my bedside lamp.

My mobile phone pinged. I sighed, hoping I wasn't going to have to enter into some lengthy texting session with someone. It was a notification from my word game to say someone had played.

The Voice had left me a chat message. They hadn't played a word yet, just left some text. I opened the little green chat bubble and read:

THE VOICE: Despot. Is that the best you can do?

CHAPTER 5

I was rudely awoken by Bob Marley and his three little birds pulsating through the house at 8.11 am. I never realised that Bob had the vocal ability to make a house shudder.

"Shit!" Realising how late I was, I unwrapped myself from my warm cocoon and scurried downstairs.

"Turn that down!" I shouted to Brendon who looked like he hadn't even moved from the Starship Enterprise where I'd left him last night. "Did you go to bed?"

"Nah, got caught up in a battle, I'll go in a bit bro."

"ERRR, we've got to be at school in 45 minutes so NO. How *stupid*. Get ready now!" I stormed out to the kitchen and flicked the kettle on. Bryony arrived downstairs, make up expertly donned, hair in a messy concoction of gorgeous (which I knew would have taken ages to perfect) and her skirt rolled up to the perfect length.

"Oh My God are you not dressed yet?" She rolled her eyes.

"Tired. Overslept. Get yourself some cereal and get some for your brother *please* and there's a fruit salad in the fridge for lunch, I've got to get ready." I grabbed my tea.

"NOW BRENDON!" I shouted as I rushed past his room.

On route to school Brendon took his lack of sleep out on Bryony. "Why have you got all that SHIT on your face? *'Ooh, My names Bryony and I have to follow what everybody else does because I can't think for myself,"* he mocked in a schoolgirl accent.

"Shut up and leave her alone," I snapped.

Bryony stuck her middle finger up at him from the back seat.

"Less of that!" I glared at her through the rear view mirror.

"Do you wanna do that again?" he threatened, twisting to look at Bryony in the back seat.

She had the sense to remain silent and I pulled up, letting her out of the car quickly near the lower school reception so she could walk with her friends. "Bye darling, see you later," I smiled. She slammed the door and scowled at her brother through the passenger side window as she walked past, pulling at her waistband to get her skirt just so.

"MARDY BITCH!" Brendon yelled through the window he had quickly zipped open, as we drove by her to the upper school. I gave him a stern look as I shut it from my control panel. I decided not to start an argument right then as we were just about to have his weekly review with the Special Educational Needs Co-ordinator(SENCO) on his behaviour and he was already on the edge of being more vile than usual.

I parked up in the school car park and made my way to the reception of Hillfields School to the lady on the desk as Brendon skipped through school via a shortcut.

"Hello Ms. Rhodes. For Mrs. Armitage?" She knew that's exactly who I was here to see because I came at the same time every week. Plus those additional days when Brendon had one of his episodes and would neither leave the school premises or attend a lesson and I was called in to assist in his removal or calm him down by phone.

"That's right." I filled in my visitors pass for the umpteenth time and made my way up to the BASE unit. The BASE was a retreat area for kids with special educational needs or behavioural issues that needed time out or had scheduled sections of their day there. Brendon had right of access as and when and would go there when he felt like it because Brendon made his own rules.

I walked in to BASE to see him, coat still on and slumped at a desk with his head down in his folded arms. Janice Armitage was sitting next to him ready with her pen and papers and going through some notes.

"He didn't go to bed last night." I said, just so she was aware that he was likely to be hideous today.

"Are you OK?" she smiled and put her head to one side as she looked up at me.

"Getting there." I pulled a chair out from the opposite desk and sat down.

"Right, well I've got the weekly report on Brendon." The report was to identify areas of both good and unacceptable behaviour. Hillfields School adopted a comments policy that rewarded '*normal*' behaviour which I had often voiced was rather ridiculous. For one, what is normal behaviour? For Brendon, his behaviour *was* normal. Between us we had formulated a reward system whereby if Brendon managed to make it through the week with very few, negative written comments or no detentions then he would have extra computer time or Janice would give him chocolate treats. The reward had to be tangible to him to be worth attaining. A firm slap on the back and a "Good on ya, kiddo!" would have meant nothing.

Mrs. Armitage pulled out the sheets of reports. The fact that there were *sheets* made me realise it wasn't going to be good.

"Unfortunately there's been a few incidents this week, some of which we've talked about on the phone, so if we can just go through some of those… Mr. Locks will be joining us in a few minutes to talk about some of them." Mr. Locks was the deputy head. He was a big jolly guy who reminded me a little of Stephen Fry. She put on her glasses and began to read:

'Ms. Limson - Brendon was constantly shouting out silly words during the lesson when they should have been revising for their additional maths GCSE exam.'

"So was Liam, so was Joe. Did they get a written comment? Err, no," said Brendon's voice from under his arms as he remained head down.

"This is about you Brendon," Mrs. Armitage replied.

"If you re-read the sentence I think you'll find the word "*They*" in it. Should give you a clue."

He had a point but it was trivial and we both ignored it.

"You know I got an A in my mock exam for maths so what's the problem?" he pushed.

"Your behaviour," I replied, nodding at Janice to continue. Brendon's intelligence was never in question. He was exceptionally clever and Mrs. Armitage believed he was bordering on genius with a photographic memory. He had insisted that all the SEN teachers take an online IQ test which proved to be a mistake as his came out twenty points higher, and that (he'd said) was even when he was rushing and not concentrating. Since then, he would never deal with substitute teachers as they weren't proper teachers in his mind and had the inability to deal with him properly. If left in a class with a sub teacher he would find their weak point, push their boundaries and have them quitting for a job in retail within minutes. Their lack of skills in managing a child like Brendon, only fed his internal, scripted belief that they were not up to the job and he would only ever entertain senior level staff.

We skipped through the other numerous, mildly rude and defiant comments. Whilst these would be considered unacceptable by usual standards they weren't that bad for a child with Aspergers or PDA and it was only the *really* awful incidents that had to be punishable. Like the one Janice read out next:

IT department: 'Brendon broke into the Impero computer system for the 7th time this year. He somehow managed to close down the whole system so it could only be controlled by him and then set to printing several copies of the World Of Warcraft book from different printers around school. When asked why he had thought it was OK to do something like this he replied, "My friends can't afford the book." Isolation issued.'

"Well, they can't!" He raised his head for the first time. "That's called being *nice* to my friends. You *said* I had to be nicer."

"But not by manipulating the whole school system and bringing it to a standstill," Janice retorted.

Mr. Locks came through the door and Brendon put his head back onto his folded arms. "Morning, morning," he gushed, " so terribly sorry for my tardiness I've been dealing with another pressing matter." He grabbed a chair and sat next to Mrs. Armitage.

We all spoke about the incidents of the week and how severe improvements needed to be made, particularly since this was GCSE year. Janice and Mr. Locks tried to explain to Brendon how his actions, particularly with the school computers, were wholly unacceptable and how he would be serving an isolation. Isolation's never worked well with Brendon. This particular punishment involved sitting in a room on your own all day long without any breaks or time outside. For people with Aspergers it bordered on torturous and served no purpose but to make them nastier and ten times more frustrated. Whilst I didn't agree with isolations, I had to accept it and support the teachers in front of Brendon to form a united front.

"I also have to inform you that Mr. Fothergill has decided that due to the nature and defiance regarding the computer incident, Brendon will now be moved straight onto governors report." Mr. Locks looked seriously toward Brendon.

This was the last thing he needed. He sat with his head in his hands breathing rapidly and staring down at the table. I felt utterly drained bar the faint onset of palpitations and it was only 9.30 am.

"You will be getting a letter from Mr. Fothergill stating that he has now moved up from deputy headmasters report onto governors report and a meeting with the governors will be called." Mr. Locks addressed me this time.

"Do I not get a say in this? How has he gone straight from deputy head to governors and missed out on headmaster report?" My words were coming out breathlessly.

"It's Mr. Fothergill's decision," Mr. Locks shrugged and tightened his lips into a non smiling, smile, "We have to get this under control because it's GCSE year and it's very important to all year elevens."

Governors report was like the last chance saloon. Three strikes and you're out. Brendon could get three strikes in half an hour. Mess that up and you're expelled. Forever. Education over.

CHAPTER 6

I finally made it to work an hour and a half after I should have been there but my boss, Colin, was cool. He really didn't look like a Colin. Colins were sensible and plaid and he was… well he was a bit edgy and soulful.

"Hey - nice of you to make it," said Johnno, the sports writer for the collective city magazines.

I fished my iPad and iPhone from my bag before I chucked it down at the leg of my desk. "Yeah well, the thing is is Johnno, I can produce ten articles in the time it takes you to do one."

I actually liked Johnno, (AKA John Smith) he was ten years my junior and I loved teasing him. He always tried to retaliate but failed. Sometimes age was a good thing. He was a great sports lover, writer and deep down, the sweetest of people. He always bought me a present from his holidays which I found endearing.

I walked up to his desk to see what he was working on and began to read it out loud to the office. "Chelsea striker, Frank Lampard reached a milestone wearing his number 8 jersey for the boys in blue when he scored his 200th goal against West Ham…"

I looked at him and faked a yawn. "That's so boring. How about spicing it up a bit? Maybe something like this: When Frank Lampard scored his 200th goal for Chelsea I was unable to peel my eyes from his bulging thigh muscles. As Torres ran over to hug him I only wished I could have been in between them like a sandwich filling. Walking from the pitch, Frank deftly removed his shirt to reveal the sweat glistening on his rippling abs and I was forced to grab the arms of my chair as my knickers were so wet, I feared sliding off the fine Natuzzi leather."

"Oh my God!" he looked shocked, " Its about SPORT not shit for wannabe WAGS!"

"I'm all for it." Monica piped up.

"Hear, Hear," said the gaggle of girls in the entertainment section.

"Keep going." Monica urged, leaning forward and sucking on her pen.

"See!" I waved my arms across the group of girls, "you're missing a whole section of readers out. I think we should swap for a week. I'll do sport and you can write about the upcoming interior trends. You need to be more creative Johnno and stop making people fall to sleep." I winked at him as I sat down and checked my phone. I noticed an indication next to my word game. I opened it up and saw 'The Voice' had played a word and left another message. I opened up the little green chat bubble.

Despot. Is that the best you can do?

Was the one I had already read. The next one said:

THE VOICE: Do you talk?

"Arsehole." I said out loud to my phone.

" Who is?" Johnno looked over at me.

"Not you. This rude person on my game." I said placing my tiles for the best possible play. I was going to nail this bastard.

"What are you playing?" Johnno stood up stretching from his hard labour on Franks milestone achievement.

"Just an online word game. Words with friends." I replied, concentrating on placing my V on the triple letter score.

"What friends?" He laughed, trying to have a dig back.

"Virtual ones. I'd introduce you but you're too boring and they probably wouldn't like you."

I placed my word for 26 points, sated in the fact that I was still in the lead. " I bet you can't even think of a seven letter word off the top of your head can you Johnno. Except for Lampard…go on say one…hurry up…well?" I kept pushing, not giving him time to answer and purposely throwing his concentration.

"Err…I don't know …there's loads." His eyes rolled up to the left searching his sporty little brain for answers.

"I've got one for you." He stared at me with a smirk, waiting for my retort.

"Dullard." The office cracked up and Johnno mouthed

a "Fuck you" at me as he returned to his desk.

I went back to my game and replied to 'The Voice' in the chat message:

SOPHISTICATION: Yes I do talk, as it happens but I usually save my wit and repartee for those not wishing to deliberately provoke me into trivial conversation. I think you don't care for the word despot because you are one.

I pressed send and felt vitriolic.

My desk phone buzzed. It was Colin. "Soph, you got a minute…?"

Colin was the only one with his own office since he was the Editor but he always had his door open and you could often hear his collection of comedy podcasts playing from within.

"Sit down babe." He fussed through some papers on his desk. He looked particularly swag today in an eclectic mix of what looked like Armani meets All Saints of Spittlefields.

"Sorry about this morning. You know how it is." I gushed whilst getting comfortable in his Eames leather chair.

"It's fine Soph, come on, you know that. How're you doing?" He looked at me with his big, soulful blue eyes.

"My life sucks. He's now on governors report for breaking into the school computer system. Sometimes I feel like letting him get chucked out of the school and learning the hard way. It's so goddam draining but I'm his Mum and it's my job is to make everything OK."

"Maybe he should work here. Could use some hackers."

"LOL" I replied sarcastically.

"Look - I need you to cover the Coconut Lounge opening tonight - Loads of people, food, wine, beer, celebs, local business - the usual. Take a friend…and I'll need some photos too and a piece from Simms the owner. I'd go with you but I've got to meet Trudie."

"Who's Trudie?"

"Ah… Some girl I met at the races event. She's nice…" he offered weakly.

"What happened to Simone? I mean, she was gorgeous!"

"You know how it is Soph." He gave a lopsided smile and tilted his head.

Colin went through girls like an addict on coke. They were always stunning and devastatingly perfect but didn't last very long. He couldn't seem to strike that magical bond with anyone.

"OK, I'll cover it. What time does it start and will Frank Lampard be there?" I asked.

"7.30 pm. Be there a bit earlier and talk to everyone. I want a a couple of pages on this. And no I doubt it…why?"

"Shame…could have taken Johnno."

We talked about the rest of the weeks magazine interior placements and I went back to my desk to see my mobile lit up. Three missed calls from Hillfields School.

"Oh God…" I groaned. I pressed return call and waited to be answered.

"Mrs. Armitage, please," I said quickly to the receptionist before she could finish her scripted delivery.

"Hi it's Sophie," I said when Janice answered.

"Oh thanks for coming back so quickly. We have a bit of a problem. He's just been removed from business studies for accessing the teachers laptop." I heard her exhale a weary sigh. "He changed the screen and then went into the teachers private documents to get information about another pupil. Furthermore he left the lesson stating he was hungry and couldn't cope and was then upset with the canteen staff for not having any bacon cobs available. He banged the finger scanner on the counter and shouted. 'For fucks sake' and frightened the canteen lady on duty. Afterwards he came to Base and demanded that I call you because he can't deal with this place." There was a pause and I felt the cramp evolving in the tightened hand around my mobile phone. "So… he's here in Base with me and very distressed. We *really* need you to fetch him if you can?"

I let out my breath, heavily. I really, *really* didn't need this. "Give me half an hour and I'll be there."

"Everything alright?" asked a concerned Johnno.

"Not really. See if you can get me a date with Frank Lampard, that might help." I patted his shoulder as I walked by him back towards Colin's office.

"Colin," He looked up from his computer and paused a Ricky Gervais podcast. "I've got to go. Schools rang… I'll need to work from home if I can?… and I can still do tonight no problem."

"Just go babe, go on. I'll call you later." He smiled sincerely. He was an awesome boss, he really was.

I arrived at Hillfields school forty minutes later and

rushed through reception holding up my visitors pass from this morning. Why I needed a visitors pass anyway was beyond me. I was there that often I should be invited to the bloody Christmas party.

Brendon was sat in The Base, head down, like earlier this morning. Janice spotted me in the corridor and rushed up to me before I opened the door and ushered me into her office.

"Thanks for coming so quickly. He seems very stressed and agitated. I think it's best he goes home. He's only going to get into more trouble and now that he's been moved onto governors report…"

"It's fine, I understand. No sleep last night won't have helped but it's impossible to make him do as he's told."

"OH I KNOW!" she gave an empathetic smile, "look, there's a governors meeting tomorrow night and Mr. Fothergill has insisted that you and Brendon attend. It's after school about 4.30pm. Brendon needs to realise how serious this is and maybe this will be the thing that makes him stop and think."

"Right. No problem. See you again tomorrow!" I replied with obvious, fake joy.

She squeezed my arm in a friendly 'I-totally-know-what-you're-going-through' way and opened the door to Brendon. When he saw me he jumped up and ran to hug me, holding on for way longer than people usually hugged for.

"Get me out of this hell hole, Mum."

CHAPTER 7

On the way home Brendon stared at the floor of the car and began to try and verbalise his feelings.

"No one understands me or how I feel. They don't tell you everything Mum, you know. It's so hard for me when they don't listen or understand and they start shouting. I don't belong and I feel awkward and it makes me angry."

"We all understand that," I said softly, " Mrs. Armitage *certainly* does because that's her job."

"NO! She might understand it a bit but SHE doesn't have Aspergers or PDA and neither do you. How can *anyone* know how I feel? Plus she's in Mr. Fothergill's gang and has to do what *he* says anyway. Sometimes I feel like killing myself. I fucking hate my life."

I stopped the car. The sentence, "I want to kill myself" are not words you want to hear coming from your troubled, teenage son.

"Brendon. If you ever feel like that you must promise to talk to me. Remember you are deeply loved and cared for by your family and friends and people around you are just trying to help you. It's going to take time. You have to find a way of fitting into the rules of life 'cos the world isn't going to change for you. I'll always be here for you. *Always.*"

"And they go on about not swearing. Like every kid swears. It's just a goddam word. They care more about that than they do about bullying or racism or drugs or starvation. The worlds fucked up man."

He had a point. Sometimes I found the way he thought refreshing and challenging. "Yes, but it's disrespectful and people find it offensive. You should be mindful not to upset other people."

We arrived home and I made him some scrambled eggs on toast and a glass of milk. He only ever drank milk.

"I'm working from home today now but I have to go out for a few hours tonight to cover an event. Are you OK with that?"

"Yo fam. Don't want your bossman givin' ya da flip homie. Dat be peak." Brendon slipped into the chav talk of his peers. He often did this just to take the piss out of people he referred to as 'wanna be gangsters and wanna be black.'

He went willingly to bed before I suggested it and I moved to my study to try and actually do some work. I emailed Colin to thank him for his understanding and that I was at my desk an on it. Then I went to try and phone Karl. It was time that Daddy gave me a hand. His phone went straight to his answer machine, "Hi this is Rhodes, Karl Rhodes, please leave your name and number and I'll get back to you ay-sap." Really? He now said it on his voice message?

"Karl its Rhodes, Sophie Rhodes. Governors meeting for your son tomorrow at 4.30pm. I'd like you to be there."

With Brendon asleep it was actually quite peaceful and easy to work from home without all the distractions and I got way more done than usual. I was kept entertained by Johnno with the occasional iMessage:

JOHN SMITH: Frank say's he's busy and he doesn't really like blondes.

SOPHIE RHODES: What a knob. Ok, try Torres.

JOHN SMITH: He's just a baby. Can you speak Spanish?

SOPHIE RHODES: He needs guidance. I don't want to talk to him.

I texted my best friend Karen to see if she wanted to come out to the Coco Lounge later and enjoy the fruits of free wine and fodder. She responded with a "I'll be at yours for 6pm and I'm gonna get pissed." Of course she was. She was a nurse, so that was a given.

I worked like a demon until 3.30 pm when Bryony and her friend Paige came home from school. She was surprised to see me back and gave me a big hug. Bryony was as bonkers as I was and probably the one person in my family who actually 'got me.'

"It's OK if Paige stays for tea, right?"

"Sure," I gave Paige a hug, " I'm going out later but I'll get you a Dominoes pizza if you like? Your brother's in bed because he got sent home so be quiet-ish."

"I heard. Didn't he smash a finger scanner in the canteen?" Paige laughed at this.

"Not quite but…along those lines. He's a bit low so be careful around him."

I felt for Bryony. Whilst she had a great bond with Brendon, an unbreakable connection, she was also subject to his wrath at any given moment. It was important that I made her free time as fun and easy as possible.

The girls helped me get ready for the party which was annoying. One was straightening my hair and the other was laying various attire on my bed. My whole wardrobe was coming out. It was decided: Skinny black jeans, Irregular Choice shoes, a nice little top from French Connection, a pale pink silk scarf and a tight leather jacket.

When I came downstairs Brendon was up and at his computer watching a Youtube video with some American guy ranting on about something.

"Your pizza will be here in about twenty minutes. Don't be long on games, you've got to be in bed at a normal time tonight, OK?"

"What time will you be back?"

"About 10pm." I heard Karen arrive in a taxi and said my goodbye's telling Bryony to call me straight away if there were any problems.

Seeing Karen was a relief. She was my oldest school friend and we reverted to stupid teenagers as soon as we met. We caught up on both our lives on the way to the Coco Lounge and I gave her a little notepad and pen and told her to listen out for any gossip whilst she was there and write it down.

We arrived outside around 7pm and the place was already filling up. I recognised some of the usual faces from other openings and suchlike. Local business men and women, magazine and newspaper journos', spies from other establishments and so on. The place was gorgeous with a simplistic rustic vibe, open brick and dark leather. The bar swept through the middle in a gentle curve of rich oak and glass and was accessible from both sides. Waiters wandered round with vol-au-vents and other pretentious finger foods and the bar was sparkling with shiny champagne glasses waiting to be filled. I took out my camera and began taking some shots before it got too crowded. The lighting was perfect and I captured some great pictures from the reflections in the huge, Italian designed, faceted mirrors.

"Champagne's out!' Karen whispered in my ear.

"Go get my friend!" I turned and watched her expertly slip through the gathering throng of merrymakers to lift the glasses.

I spied Simms, the owner talking to the Paul Hymes, director at Ferrari near the end of the bar. I mooched over ready to get in and ask him some questions. I knew Paul as did most people in the city, noted for his Ferrari 458 Spider adorned with his '*HYM3S*' private number plate and the fact he was a lecherous old sod.

"Sophie darling!" he shmoozed as I approached. He held out his arm to collect me into his space. He smelt of Bollinger and Davidoff Cool Water.

"Paul my darling," I sang with as much pathetic gushiness as I could muster. I tried not to visibly cringe as he ran his hand down my back. Whilst I thought he was a prick I had to resist from saying so. Firstly I would lose my job and secondly you never knew if there was chance of a Ferrari in the offing. Having said that, I doubted you would get one without shagging him in the back seat of his. We made small talk and enthused about the venue and Paul kept filling my glass as I tried to ask Simms about the bar and his forthcoming ideas. Suddenly a group of promotion girls from the local radio came over dressed in black leather, with smoky eyes and tousled locks. It was like an audition for Cat Woman. Fortuitously, it took Paul's attention away from me and I was able to slip away unnoticed and join my nearly plastered friend. I found her talking to some guys from the nearby vodka bar. Though I'd joined the conversation late I already ascertained that they'd figured out she was a nurse and were telling her tales of their mate getting his bollocks stuck in his flies and ending up at A&E.

I checked my phone and read the following texts:

COLIN FRAY: How's it going Soph?

JOHN SMITH: Is Frank there? I told him you were going…

I replied to both and took the opportunity to text Karl. He'd not called me back yet.

> *KARL - Please let me know that you're coming tomorrow. Really important and need your backup.*

I clicked on my word game whilst the story of one man and his trapped balls continued.

> *THE VOICE: How do you know that the conversation would be frivolous. We have yet to have one.*

I noticed he'd played a storming word attached to another and scoring 33 points. Bastard.

> *SOPHISTICATION: Well I can't say you've inspired to me to start one.*

The rest of the night was fun and easy and we chatted with lots of different people. For the first time in a long while I laughed and drank and felt some freedom from my fractured life. My feet, however, were starting to throb wildly. NB: do not ever listen to teenagers again on what to wear. Irregular Choice heels should only be worn when going out to sit down. i.e.: Dining.

I beckoned my party to a nearby table that had just been vacated and fell into the seat, kicking off my heels and placing my angry feet on the cool tiled floor. Bliss. It was then that I felt the buzz of my phone in my pocket. I reached into the tight opening and fished it out. Twelve missed calls from Brendon.

"Shit." I excused myself and forced my swollen feet back into the shoes from hell. I felt like an ugly sister with a glass slipper as I teetered outside like a newly born deer so I'd be able to hear him. He answered immediately. I barely heard it ring.

"WHERE THE FUCK ARE YOU?"

"Err, watch how you speak to me please!" I felt the cheer and easiness of the evening drain away like a plug had been pulled.

"WHERE ARE YOU?"

"I'm out working REMEMBER." I said sternly.

"But it's 10.33"

"So?"

"You said you'd be back at 10 pm. You're 33 minutes late already and I've been looking for you since then."

"10…10.30…what does it matter. I said around 10 pm"

"You SAID 10! Can you please come home NOW."

"FINE!" I ended the call and made a mental note to self: Do not be specific in future. Be vague and remember that what you say to Brendon will always be taken literally.

I left Karen at the party with the vodka barons after explaining my dilemma. She totally understood, she was his Godmother and because of me she'd never had kids.

Getting a cab home was easy as it was midweek and I was home at just after 11pm.

Every light in the house was on and Brendon was

peering out from behind the heavy, tapestry curtains awaiting my arrival.

"*EVENTUALLY,*" his eyes were black and I felt his dark mood permeating the air like poisonous sludge.

"Yes, I'm back now, so leave it there. Where's Bryony?"

"She was in bed watching vampire shit. I've been on my own wanting to go to bed for ages. If I'm tired tomorrow it's your fault." He glared at me, the underlying threat of misbehaving tomorrow hanging there as a punishment for my lateness.

"Then go to bed. Because I am." I kicked my shoes off at the bottom of the stairs and he violently kicked them out of his way as he stomped up them. He'd managed to assert his control and now he would hopefully sleep.

"Goodnight Brendon, love you," I sang as I passed by his door after checking on a sleeping Bryony.

"Night," he mumbled, grudgingly.

Chapter 8

I woke up with a *'I'm-never-drinking-wine-or-champagne-again'* headache and if you could take the smell of an old, wet dog and put it in my mouth, I'm sure that's what it would taste like. It was relatively early and still dark outside so I made use of the stillness and went downstairs to get a cup of tea and two paracetamol. I sat quietly and wished I could just have one day a week that was like this. Peace. Solitude.

I spent the next ten minutes mulling over the previous night and wondering how the hell Karen must be feeling when I remembered it was the governors meeting later today. I still hadn't heard from Karl. Damn him. I went back to my bedroom and checked my phone. Nothing except for five emails from Living Social and Groupon. It was only 6.45 am but I decided to ring anyway. Karl was one of those annoying, chirpy, morning people.

"Good morning!" he boomed, his phone obviously attached to his car audio as I could hear the rumblings of the motorway behind him.

"Why haven't you responded to my call and text about

this school meeting?" I asked holding the phone an inch away from my ear in fear of perforation.

"Ah, I had every intention of doing so but I have meetings all over the place and not sure if I can change them. I was going to call later when I've seen what I can do."

"But this is important. You know what Mr. Fothergill's like and I don't want to face a whole bunch of governors on my own. He's going to get kicked out if we don't fight his corner."

"Look, if I can, I'll be there but I'm not promising. I have to work and can't pander to the school every time Brendon has an outburst. They need to get a grip on controlling it or he needs to learn a hard lesson and face the consequences of his actions."

"Righto, Daddy dearest," I checked my attitude quickly. I wanted him there so needed to play nice. "Look, I'd really appreciate it and I understand what you're saying. I could do with your people skills and expertise in argumentation and negotiation." I went straight to the ego. Always works.

"I'll do my best and I'll call you later," he rounded up, ready to go but I knew he'd now feel more compelled to turn up.

I got Brendon and Bryony up and fed and managed to stop a huge fight where Bryony had nearly worn her Ready Brek on her face for calling Brendon a douche bag. Thankfully it made a turnabout into brother and sister unite when I went mad- bitch- crazy and started yelling at the pair of them.

"You two are so BLOODY SELFISH! I don't need this crap in the morning. I've got to get to work and I've lots to do and your trivialities and arguing can STOP NOW! I *don't* CARE if you think Bryony's friends are a bunch of *hapless skets* with no brain cells,'" I directed at Brendon. "And *you,* Bryony, shouldn't give a flying banana if he thinks that anyway because you KNOW he's a chauvinistic, arrogant and opinionated swine!" I snatched away the breakfast plates and wondered if I was having a brain haemorrhage. My head was pounding so hard and I wanted hurt someone.

"Are you on your period?" said Brendon.

Bryony burst out laughing. "I know right?"

"GET. IN. THE. CAR." I glared at them.

On the way to school I gave Brendon a lecture. "Listen, it's the meeting after school. Your Dad might be coming too. Maybe. Can you *please,* for just one day *NOT* break into any computers and actually behave yourself. When we're in the meeting, be polite, do NOT get annoyed and let me or Dad do the talking." I looked at him rolling his eyes at Bryony, "I'm DEADLY serious. This is not a joke and if you don't start towing the line you'll be expelled."

"Yes Mommy," he mocked in a brat voice.

They got out and wandered down the street collecting friends. Brendon grabbing one of his in a bear hug since he was one of the biggest in the year and used his physical strength as a way of control. I drove to work playing Classic FM in order to zen myself out.

I arrived before time and got straight into loading and editing photos. By the time everybody else started to appear I was well into my Coco Lounge article.

"Good night?" asked Johnno as he slapped his Adidas sports bag on the desk.

"Good morning," I replied not looking up and trying not to break my roll.

"Ha ha. OK...*did* you have a good time last night Soph?"

"Splendid. You were sorely missed."

The day continued in a super productive manner despite the pain in my temples refusing to take leave. I even rewrote my article three times over because Colin wanted to move things about and have more photos, less text. Then more text. Ugh. Then there wasn't room for the book review so all the layout had to be re arranged. By the time the afternoon came I was desperately in need of a nap.

"Johnno, you know you want to go to Starbucks and get me a caramel latte and a muffin," I pleaded.

"No. That stuff's bad for you. He reached into his drawer and threw a muesli health bar at me. "Have that instead."

"Ugh. Damn you sporty types. Have you no soul?"

"I'm heading out in a minute," said Monica, "I'll bring the carbs back for you."

"Thank you FRIEND." I blew her a kiss.

"Hey, how's the arsehole?" asked Johnno.

"Which one?" I asked puzzled, notching them up in my mind.

"The one on the game."

"Well let me see…" I picked up my phone and clicked on Word.

THE VOICE: You need to be inspired to start a conversation? How interesting. Are you that easy to annoy?

"Yep. Still an arsehole," I replied. However I was starting to find The Voice somewhat intriguing.

SOPHISTICATION: You're not annoying me, though I've no doubt that's your intention. I just happen to find you amusing.

Like I would give him the satisfaction of thinking he'd annoyed me. I had mostly vowels which didn't help with my desperate need for victory. He was twelve points ahead. Not good. As I was playing around with my letters the little green chat bubble delivered a new message. Well, looky, looky 'The Voice' was awake and live online.

THE VOICE: Amusing? What, like a monkey?

SOPHISTICATION: Yes. Like a monkey.

I played my pathetic vowels for 14 points.

THE VOICE: You really aren't trying very hard are you.

SOPHISTICATION: With this conversation with a monkey or with my play?

THE VOICE: Either.

It suddenly occurred to me that I was assuming 'The Voice' was male. Just because they were rude and belligerent that shouldn't make me assume it was a man.

SOPHISTICATION: What gender are you?

THE VOICE: Rare and amusing male monkey.

That actually made me smile.

THE VOICE: Are you really sophisticated or is that just something you aspire to be because you're not amusing like me?

SOPHISTICATION: Yes I am, as it happens.

THE VOICE: I'll take your word for it. I must leave now and go to work.

SOPHISTICATION: Well I must leave now and finish work.

I closed the game and wondered where The Voice lived if he was only just starting his day.

I noticed my latte and muffin had been put on my desk. I reached for the polystyrene beaker and poured the sweet coffee into my mouth, begging that the caffeine would have some magic cure on my sore head.

My phone beeped with a text from Karen:

Just got up. Dying. Didn't get in until 4 am. Drunk as a fucking Lord. Thank God not at work today as would vomit on patients, though could do with raiding the hospital meds cabinet for some serious pain relief. Hurts to even blink. BTW - Vodka boys are planning a big come back and buying that old cafe next door - it's all hush hush but of course I was going to tell you. Ring me when I'm better. About 5 days. x

SOPHIE RHODES: And you wonder why nurses get such a bad rep ;) Thanks for the inside info. You can always work here! x

Brilliant. I rushed in to Colin's office and told him about the piece of gossip. "Send one of Monica's girls in later to find out. I'd go but my head hurts and I've got to leave now for the *big* school meeting. Wish me luck. "

"I expect nothing less than victory for Brendon and if they don't play nice tell 'em we'll be writing about their discrimination against children with disabilities."

"Nice!" I gave him a high five and left for the Hillfields

School. As I approached my car, I tried to ring Karl again as he hadn't got back to me as promised.

"On my way. Be there near half four," he answered.

I let go of the breath I hadn't realised I was holding.

"Thank God. Ok well put your foot down it starts at 4.30 pm." I knew he would because he had a bright yellow, Volvo T5 and he couldn't help but pretend he was Ayrton Senna. And Bond of course, James Bond.

CHAPTER 9

As I pulled into the car park I saw Karl's shiny, yellow car and breathed a sigh of relief. I parked my filthy, pale blue, mini cooper next to it and wished I'd asked Paul Hymes for a loan of a Ferrari.

I scurried into reception and saw Karl sitting there suited and booted and enveloped in a dark grey, cashmere overcoat. He certainly looked the part. We didn't look like parents who tolerated thuggery and outlandish behaviour from our offspring.

"Thanks for coming, it is appreciated." I sat down next to him and he handed me a visitors pass. It was odd seeing my name in his writing. I'd forgotten what it looked like and my stomach lurched from the memory.

"So…Fill me in," he said, turning toward me slightly.

I explained that Brendon had been breaking into computers, being defiant and rude as usual, playing rough shod with his mates in the hallways etc. I explained that Mr. Fothergill had put him on governors report and this was his last chance. Karl and I both despised Mr. Fothergill. He was like a politician and loved the sound of his own voice. He was only interested in results that made him and his school look good and seemed to have very little empathy with pupils. He didn't want Brendon in his school, that was obvious and in many respects I understood why not. Nobody needs a kid like Brendon spoiling the creamery and going round the school like a whirling dervish. However, the school got money for supporting and including children with disabilities and it would be difficult for him to get rid of Brendon without doing it properly.

Janice Armitage appeared in reception. " They're ready for you now."

We followed her upstairs where we met Brendon at the top. He gave his Dad a courteous nod and Karl patted his shoulder.

"Make sure you behave in here," I whispered as I sidled next to him.

We entered the board room, where situated around a large oval table sat Mr. Fothergill and his secretary, Mr. Locks the deputy head plus two ladies and a man who I surmised were 'The Governors'. The rest of us walked in and took our seats.

"Good afternoon," said Mr. Fothergill. "If everyone can introduce themselves round the table for the purpose of the minutes." Mr. Fothergill looked just like Neil Tenant (present day version) from The Pet Shop Boys sans musical personality. We went around the table saying our names out loud. "Sophie Rhodes, Mother." I announced hoping Karl wouldn't do his James Bond thing and look a pillock. "Karl Rhodes, Father," he said. Phew, thank God.

"Brendon Rhodes, fugitive," said Brendon stoically. Really? Now he wants to be funny? I noticed two of the governors smile at his reply and thanked God they had a sense of humour.

"Brendon, please remove your coat," demanded Mr. Fothergill.

"I'd rather not, I'm cold."

I kicked Brendon under the table and sweetly said, " Take your coat off, darling," whilst giving him that '*I-swear-to God-I'll -kill-you-if-you-start*' look.

He took it off.

"Right, well I think myself, Mrs. Armitage and Mr. Locks will take turns in going through the issues and incidents of late from the reports and comments from staff." Mr. Fothergill continued. "The nature of the incidents to be discussed were serious enough for me to place Brendon immediately onto governors report. After we have highlighted the incidents both the governors and Mr. and Ms. Rhodes can respond." He looked at us all for confirmation. I wanted to stick my tongue out at him but I nodded politely. There was something about him that made me revert to child. Some teachers seemed to do that to you and make you feel really nervous and inadequate which was ridiculous. I was used to big meetings, press conferences and bullshitters and could generally hold my own in most situations but this one made me feel about six years old. Thankfully, Karl didn't have that problem. Nor did Brendon which *was* the problem.

Mr. Locks started. "Unfortunately there have been a

plethora of incidents, some minor like rough play in the corridors with friends and having his phone out in school but the few I'd like to concentrate on are these:" He lifted up the report sheets. I got my pen and notebook ready to make crucial notes.

Media: Miss Brown - Brendon told me he could not log onto the school computer because he had forgotten his password. I said he would have to use paper for the lesson. He said "No, that's antiquated can you please get my computer open." When I refused he responded with, "How long have you been teaching at this school and you still don't know how to do that?" I asked Brendon to be quiet but he refused and persisted challenging my decision. I told him to settle or he would be asked to leave. He refused, and I said I would call for someone to remove him. He said, "Fine. Make the call." I called for Mr Fearon to remove Brendon. On the way out of the class he came over to me and said, " You have been in a bad mood with me for, let's see, about a week now. This suggests you might have some personal issues. I don't think you should be letting your personal issues affect your teaching of this lesson." I found his comments of a derogatory nature.

Miss Harris: I entered L15 and found Brendon and another boy playing with a football. I confiscated the ball and Brendon looked at me, smiled and clicked his fingers and pointed at my face. I told him not to do that. He replied "God, you're miserable." I told him that was rude and he said, "No, perceptive." His comments were very personal.

"There is also the incident involving the Imperio computer system which is what has had Brendon step up to the level of governors report; he shut down the whole system and tried to print several books from the internet," he finished.

I looked around the table and one of the governors was shaking her head.

Janice Armitage took over from there. "Well Brendon *has* had some positive comments too, one from Miss. Bench from French." I tried not to snigger at this and put my hand over my mouth. 'Miss. Bench from French' the one with the stacked top shelf as it were. No doubt he behaved in *that* lesson.

"There's also one from Design Technology…Mr. Green, who says Brendon was very helpful in bringing all the woodworking tools to the classroom." I looked over at him wondering if he'd half inched a chisel or something. Brendon had a thing for destructive tools.

"We are working very closely with Brendon on his social interaction and what is and isn't appropriate and have set aside a little more time in BASE to have one to one time with him." She stopped and nodded towards Mr. Fothergill.

Mr. Fothergill took a deep breath, lifted his notes and tapped them on the table to straighten them. He thanked Mr. Locks and Mrs. Armitage for their input before his analysis.

"Apart from the very serious incidents that we've just

heard about there are several other minor events where Brendon is quite rough around school, play fighting with friends, which can be very intimidating for other pupils as well as staff." He looked pointedly at Brendon. "Because of his pertinent attitude and remarks of a personal nature to staff, including swearing at dinner ladies, he has, in the space of one month, been issued with seven detentions and an isolation. His behaviour has got to change drastically, particularly now we are in GCSE year. Abusing the schools computer system is certainly something that will not be tolerated and due to this, I would like Brendon to remain on governors report for the next six weeks with a review at another scheduled meeting to see if he has met with the sanctions."

I looked at the half scribbled notes in my book: Computers, Mr. Fothergill's tie - *hideous,* passwords and other starred, blank lines waiting to be filled along with mindless drawings I'd done of circles and triangles. Completely useless and not to my usual note taking standard.

The governors were then asked to give their thoughts. Mr. Smith introduced himself; the only male governor. He had a kind open face and I liked him before he even opened his mouth. "Well, now we've heard some of the incidents I'd like to get an idea of how Brendon feels about them." He spoke calmly and with a smile as he looked over at Brendon, who raised his eyes to meet his for a split second before going back to the piece of paper he'd been making into some sort of origami concoction. "And of course, from Mr. and Ms. Rhodes on their thoughts," he continued. Yes. I liked him. I drew a little star next to his name on my notes.

"If you don't mind Mr. Smith," interrupted the lady governor, who'd been shaking her head and looking like a cantankerous shrew, " before that, I'd like to know why this young man here hasn't even *flinched* at the mention of all these detentions and from where I'm sitting, has shown *very* little remorse and not *once* lifted his head up and given any eye contact!"

I looked at the lady governor dumbfounded and then at Karl who moved uncomfortably in his seat. Brendon looked briefly around, then at me, and then back to tearing up his paper toy.

She leant forward, directly opposite Brendon, peering through her gold rimmed, glasses at him. She was around sixty -ish with dark grey hair, wound in a tight bun which fitted neatly into the nape of her neck and sported a crisp, white blouse. Old school. Straight out of a Dickens novel.

A moment of over stretched silence hit the room as we all, but Brendon, looked on at her.

"You *do* understand Aspergers?" Karl directed at her.

"I'm asking that your *child* answer, Mr. Rhodes, and please look at me when I'm addressing him," she stated.

"Clearly not then, Mrs…?"

"Johnstone, Mrs. Johnstone. I introduced myself earlier," she retorted firmly.

"If you were familiar with the condition Aspergers, Mrs. Johnstone, then you'd be aware that a child with this *'disability,'* he emphasised, "will not look you directly in the eyes when talking to you as they find it intimidating."

"Regardless, its common manners and I'd like his response to the level of detentions he has acquired," she clipped.

"Brendon," I looked over to him and smiled. "Please can you tell this lady how you feel about the amount of detentions you've had."

He looked at me and then at her, flitting between us as he answered. "I don't feel anything...I don't know what you mean..."

"Do you not see this as *quite* outrageous to be punished this often?" she asked.

"Not really, I don't always think I should have a detention, not for the little things that I don't think are bad." He continued shredding his paper more ferociously.

"And what about the comments you make to teachers? Do you not think they're inappropriate?"

"I'm only saying what I think."

"Well let me tell you what I think: I think you are a rude and defiant young man who is discrediting this school. You are lucky to be getting an education and good teachers and all you seem to be doing is making a mockery of it all with your *outlandish* and difficult behaviour.'

I saw Mr. Fothergill nod in agreement. I wanted to smack him in the face. Before either Karl or I could interject Brendon spoke up for himself.

"Look, I don't know what it is you don't get but I don't see detentions as bad. Like, they don't bother me. I get them all the time because no one understands me and even if I try to explain it to teachers they say '*I'm arguing*' and I just get another one. I mean, do you *really* think I WANT to be like this?" He actually did look her directly in the eye when he said that. "Do you think I want to have Aspergers? I want to be like every other kid and be able to sit still and get on with work and understand people but I can't and I can't change it."

My heart melted and I wanted to gather him in my arms and take him far, far away from this nightmare situation. I saw empathy in the eyes of the other two governors but not of the old shrew. She remained staunchly hard faced.

"Brendon," said Mr. Smith, "thanks for telling us that and we will take that on board, of course. Now if we can move over to Mr. & Ms. Rhodes and have their thoughts." He smiled warmly in our direction.

Karl looked over at me to see if I wanted to go first. I looked down at my notes…hmm…they weren't much help. "Well," I started, trying to run events through my mind, "obviously I'm concerned and upset that Brendon has been moved onto this level of report but I am well aware that the computer incident is totally unacceptable and I have spoken to Brendon about this. As for the other incidents, well, I don't think some of them are relevant like 'horse play' with your friends. That's just normal, teenage boy behaviour, surely?" I looked for agreement in the sea of faces but didn't find it. "The inappropriate responses, well, that's part and parcel of the condition but something both Mrs. Armitage and I are dealing with together. I do come in to school regularly to meet up with the SEN team and working as a united front seems to help." It was weak but I wanted them to understand that I was doing my level best to keep him walking within the walls of acceptance.

"Well it doesn't appear to be helping very well Ms. Rhodes," Mrs. Johnstone replied with a condescending smirk on her face.

I felt like a berated school child and coloured slightly at her remark.

"Are you aware of how difficult this is for me?" I asked looking at her and around the room at the others. "You talk to me as though I'm not making any effort. I leave my job early or get in late so that I can get to this school and help out *and* I try my hardest to support the teachers as well as my son in the education system. I don't know if you're aware but I have two children in this school. My daughter is a model student, certainly not discrediting, and has an exemplary record. She is in all the top sets, is polite, and very popular with both her peers and her teachers. Now, the *interesting* thing is, both my son and daughter have been parented in exactly the same way. I know how to bring my children up properly with manners and morals and respect for others. The difference is, one of them has Aspergers and PDA."

They all looked on waiting for me to continue but I really didn't know where else to go. Janice looked at me with softness in her eyes. She was the only one that understood the hell I went through at home and also the only one who dealt with Brendon on a day to day basis at school. She understood Aspergers whereas the rest of them clearly didn't and probably didn't really care.

"If I may pick up from there," Karl interjected, saving me from my predicament. "We are very understanding of the schools policies and the necessity to have this school running smoothly and without severe incidents that will impact on other students and teachers. I work in the corporate field and am well versed on how structure and maintaining good relationships works. What you *fail* to take into any consideration, is Brendon's condition. You are sitting here with Brendon's behavioural plan in front of you, advising how he 'should' be treated within a lesson. Have you all read that?" He looked pointedly at Mr. Fothergill and the shrew who remained visibly untouched. The others shuffled through their papers to locate it. "Allow me to remind you," he continued, raising the plan to read. "You will note on this plan that it clearly states that Brendon will not look directly in your eyes as he will find this intimidating. *It states* that he will find it difficult to sit still and focus. *It states* that he will sometimes need to leave a lesson if highly anxious and be allowed to go straight to BASE. *It states* that he WILL, at times, make inappropriate remarks due to his lack of social skills." He placed the plan back on the table. "This is a plan that goes out to every member of staff does it not?" He looked at Mr. Fothergill for a response.

"That's correct," he replied.

"Then as head of this school and management leader I think you should insist that some of your staff *actually* read it. I would also suggest that you, yourself read it and make sure that as Head of this school you are fully converse in the field of autism, for the sake of all students on the spectrum, and that your staff are better trained in this area. There is no point to this piece of paper," he pushed it forward on the table, "If nobody but the SEN team are reading it."

"We are continually training our staff in this area and our SEN team work very hard with children who have behaviour issues," Fothergill responded.

"Well it doesn't appear to be working very well." He glanced over at Mrs. Johnstone as he used her words against her. "I have seen repeated remarks on these reports from teachers picking fault with usual autistic traits. Only quite recently, Mr. Fothergill, one of your senior members of staff had to be told to stop any interaction with Brendon as she seemed to find fun in deliberately goading him."

Ah, Miss. Raven. What an evil woman. She had constantly picked on Brendon and deliberately got him into trouble by forcing him to react. We had insisted that the school had stopped her interacting with him in any way as he used to come back home crying about her nearly every night and refusing to go to school.

"I have been summoned to a meeting, without official written notice to myself or Sophie, where you have placed our son on governors report. If I am being brought to a meeting which is about my son's behaviour, then at the very least, I expect a team of governors and teachers that have an understanding of Aspergers and PDA. Clearly that is not the case and therefore we are not at a level playing field. I will accept that the computer incident is punishable and unacceptable; I will accept that some of the comments from Brendon need addressing and working on, which is an ongoing trial for both the SEN team and Brendon's Mother. I will not, however, accept this as an official meeting. Please be sure to make that *very* apparent in the minutes." He smiled and nodded over at the secretary. "I would suggest that we all stop now and re-schedule when you have got this properly organised and we can discuss the governor's sanctions then. Please be aware that I will not remain present at any future meetings if anyone on this team has not considered my sons condition appropriately. If I suspect any further discrimination against disability, I will have no hesitation in taking this to the next level."

Karl stood up and gently pushed my shoulder to indicate it was time to leave. I raised myself from the chair and told Brendon to put his coat on. I felt very awkward but also relieved.

"Thank you everyone for your time and I look forward to the first official meeting soon." He slowly and calmly adjusted his suit jacket and put on his overcoat before walking over to shake Mr. Fothergill's hand. The Head was ever the politician and calmly took Karl's hand as he stood but I couldn't help but notice the stewing resentment behind his eyes.

We walked out of the room and down the stairs in silence. When we got to the car park I let out the longest sigh of relief and Brendon turned to his Father and said, "Owned Dad, you totally owned them. That was joke."

CHAPTER 10

Karl had certainly bought us some time if nothing else and his points at the meeting were well justified. I wanted to hug him but instead I squeezed his arm and said, "That was brilliant, thanks so much."

"Not really, they need to get their act together. It's just Fothergill trying to strong arm Brendon out and without just cause he's going to fail." He smiled and winked. "Look, there's no point me driving down south now, not on a Friday afternoon in rush hour, I'll just be stuck in traffic for hours. Do you want to go out for something to eat?"

"Err, yeah, sure...Brendon?" I looked to see if he might want to join us. Brendon didn't really do family social outings, not without causing a ruckus and after the meeting I didn't think he'd be in a sociable mood.

"Nah, I'm good," he shrugged, "I've got to go out anyway, I'm going to Luke's house."

"OK, well don't be late. Enjoy yourself." I gave him a hug and was glad that he seemed so calm and relaxed. "We'll go through all the meeting points on Sunday."

The school always seemed to hold big meetings or dish out hideous punishments on a Friday night. Just in time for the weekend, they'd send your kid home wound like a Duracell bunny and make your weekend a complete disaster. I was convinced that they did this on purpose as a get back.

I dropped Brendon at Luke's house and drove home to fetch Bryony. Karl was already outside in his car making phone calls to work on his mobile. I indicated that I'd be five minutes with a show of fingers and went inside. It was a painful reminder to see his car on the drive. Just something so simple brought forth a rush of emotions that I seemed to have buried somewhere deep within my soul.

I had already texted Bryony to get ready before I left *knowing* that she'd want to take forever to get dressed in case she was *'seen'* by some fit lad from school. Miraculously, she was already donned in her disco pants and thrift shop 70's shirt when I walked through the door.

"Don't you feel weird going out with Dad?"

"My whole life is weird Bry. I'd be concerned if something normal actually happened." I rushed upstairs to freshen up and change my skirt to Jeans.

We made our way in Karl's beast of a car to the Baltimore Diner on the edge of the canal. We discussed the meeting in parts and also Brendon's behaviour at home as we devoured insanely large onion rings and burgers drenched in smokey BBQ sauce. The conversation was difficult and over polite and I felt like we were skirting around the houses, avoiding the real issues we had once lived together. Bryony was a welcome distraction and we turned to focus on her and the dramas of life as a teenage girl as we munched our way through our American style cheesecake.

On the way back home Bryony asked if she could have a sleepover at one of her friends and Karl dropped her off before we arrived back home. There was an awkwardness between us when she'd left the car that was impossible to shift so we masked it with trivial, unnecessary chat. I'd been with this man for years and now I couldn't even talk to him normally. As soon as we pulled up on the drive, Brendon came running out of the house and opened the passenger door.

"I've made you both some cake!" he exclaimed, "come on, come and eat it, quick!"

I was so full up after the meal the last thing I wanted was more cake. However, the fact that he'd made something and was so proud meant I was going to eat it and wax lyrical about it regardless.

"You'll have to come in and eat some or he'll be upset…" I looked across at Karl whose engine was still running, ready to leave.

He turned off the ignition without making eye contact and we made our way into the house.

"I thought you were at Luke's? And since when do you make cake?" I laughed as Brendon was clumsily cutting sections of some brown stodge and putting it on delicate, floral plates.

"Yeah, that's what me and Luke were doing at his house, making cakes *Mommy*," he said in his put on American accent. "And they taste just like buttermilk biscuits," he drawled on in some southern, hillbilly fashion. "Now go and sit down and I'll bring them through." He was remarkably chipper, I noted.

Karl and I made our way to the lounge and sat down on the sofa awaiting our prize. Karl didn't remove his coat. I knew he'd want to take off as soon as he'd finished.

Brendon came through, proudly carrying two plates with a chocolate slab of cake covered in single cream.

"Eat your heart out Gordon Ramsey!" I said, thinking how sweet and kind he could be. He sat down on the arm of the sofa and waited eagerly for us to start eating it in his usual controlling manner. Karl spooned some into his mouth first and pulled an interesting face. I immediately went to taste mine so I could say how marvellous it was but…it wasn't. It tasted kind of odd.

"Mmmm, it's nice darling," I lied. "What is it exactly?…it has an unusual flavour." I carried on eating it and tried to swallow quickly without chewing too long so I could get it over with. Karl was doing the same and giving me that 'WTF?' look.

"Exactly what is this Brendon, it has a very weird taste?" I was slightly concerned because you couldn't fully trust the hygiene of teenage boys. You never knew what they might have been playing with before they went into celebrity chef mode.

"Did you both wash your hands before you made this?" I stopped mid spoonful as I stared at him. Karl had already finished his and put his plate on the coffee table.

"YES! OH.MY.GOD. Mum, just *eat* it. You're such a control freak!"

I finished it off and decided to make a cup of tea to wash the peculiar taste away and hope to God I wasn't about to get food poisoning.

"I'll make you a drink," said Brendon uncharacteristically. "You two just sit down and get ready to kiss the sky."

"What's going on Brendon?" I asked sternly, not liking his weird behaviour.

"That cake you've both just eaten is a hash brownie." He roared with laughter. "There's some serious skunk in there and you are *so* going to be able to chill out and relax for once!"

I looked at Karl and Karl looked at me. We then looked at Brendon with utter disbelief.

"Come again?" I said, "hash brownie? A HASH BROWNIE? Are you *GODDAM* KIDDING ME?! PLEASE TELL ME THIS IS A JOKE AND YOU HAVEN'T JUST DRUGGED YOUR PARENTS…"

"Don't worry, it'll take about half an hour to work and you'll feel great. Chill out man! You both need to," Brendon stated, with no concern or remorse at what he'd just done.

"Brendon…I CANNOT believe you have done this to me…I really can't…what the hell?" I gushed, trying to think. "Since when have you been taking Marijuana? Seriously…You know, YOU, the child who wouldn't even entertain Ritalin because it masks your real personality. The one who is always telling me that alcohol is bad, and fatty foods and you should train hard and look after your body. Now you think this is OK? So now you do drugs?"

"And," Karl interjected, "I am supposed to be driving home – did that cross your mind? Now I can't go anywhere. You're an idiot." The darkness filling his eyes brought back the memories of the violent outbursts between them and I froze for a moment, waiting for the explosion.

"CALM DOWN. Sheesh." Brendon threw his arms in the air, trying to diffuse the situation. "And this is the problem: the war on drugs. Actually Mother I only have it now and then, which is a lot less than most people. All teenagers at school are doing it. It doesn't hurt you, it's not addictive, and no one has ever died from it. Not like they do with alcohol or tobacco which IS legal. DUH. You don't get aggressive, like with alcohol, you just get happy and chilled. How is that bad? Anyway, I knew you'd react like this so I've sent some links to your e mail from YouTube, Harvard scientists, Reddit, and 'The Amazing Atheist'. Shit, that dude is awesome!"

This is what he did to me. Always a step ahead of the game and bombarding me with information to support his crazy actions so I couldn't argue from the seat of my pants.

"IT IS STILL AN ILLEGAL DRUG. HELLO!" I shouted, "AND I DO NOT WANT YOU TAKING IT. END OF. AND I CERTAINLY DON'T WANT YOU DRUGGING ME FOR YOUR OWN ENTERTAINMENT PURPOSES. YOU'RE THE CONTROL FREAK!"

"It's legal in Colorado and California," he justified.

"This is ENGLAND not Hollywood!"

"Well, it should be legal. So should prostitution, cocaine…anything. It's peoples free choice. Taking away freedom is bad. There'd be a lot more money if the government legalised weed and put tax on it. There'd be more jobs, more money for health centres, less money spent on policing petty drug crimes. Pound for pound, marijuana costs more than gold, so think about it. Read all the information and understand the facts before you start going psycho."

"Freedom? Oh freedom! Right! What about MY FREE WILL? Oh wait…YOU just took that away by giving me WHACKY CAKE!" I retorted.

Karl lifted his hand to indicate he wanted to speak, like we were in a board meeting or something. "Legalising drugs is a ridiculous idea and only something a nearly sixteen year old would say. Marijuana is a gateway drug for a start. What next Brendon? Ecstasy? Cocaine? If we legalise any drug you'd have a bunch of muppets who never did anything in the country." Karl removed his coat and pinched the top of his nose with his thumb and forefinger. I knew he was getting annoyed but now it was not his place to start a fight in our home.

"You're living in the dark ages Dad, get on the RIGHT side of history." He shook his head and left the room.

"I can't believe he's done this." I looked at Karl who was rubbing his hand across his mouth and developing that tight, mean look on his face.

"I'm going to have to stay here now." He looked over

at me with raised eyebrows to question if that was going to be alright. "I can't feel it working yet though, maybe I'll be immune to it."

"Yeah, that's fine…did you have plans tonight?" I felt terribly guilty and parentally inadequate. "I can't feel anything either but then I never did when I was younger and tried it."

In my past I'd often had a draw on some boyfriends' roach at a party but had never experienced that cool and easy reggae vibe that everyone else did. I think I was just too hyperactive and the nearest thing to have possibly got me into that state would be getting shot with a wild animal tranquilliser.

"No plans especially." We both sat there for several minutes in silence, shell-shocked and awaiting some sort of revelation.

And then it happened.

I felt the faint onset of nausea. A wave of something taking hold and denying my body the ability of control.

"Oh God, I feel sick…"

I stood up and my legs began to tremble. I tried to make my way to the kitchen and I felt as though I was walking on sponge. I stamped my feet harder on the carpet to try and make the feeling disappear but it didn't work. I was getting hot and flustered and the palpitations were doing Zumba in my chest.

"Whoa…I don't like it, I don't like it…" I clasped my

hands to my ears because I felt I could hear the ocean. What? "I'm going to KILL him!" I made my way delicately through the lounge.

Once in the kitchen I felt incredibly weird, like I might possibly faint, or even worse, die. Standing was proving difficult and I was unsure if I was about to do an Exorcist special and projectile vomit everywhere. If I was going to, it will be on Brendon I thought spitefully. I decided to lie on the floor in case death was imminent and as I placed my face on the cool tiles I felt a rush of dizziness, so I shut my eyes, ready to meet my maker.

Several minutes later I was being shaken awake by Brendon. "Mum, MUM! Wake up! You can't go to sleep. It will make you feel ill." He pulled at my top to try and raise me to a sitting position.

I looked up at him from the floor where I lay. "You're the spawn of the devil," I tried to focus on his face, "AND I'm not the devil." I added. I could vaguely make out Karl standing in the background, laughing like a child. "YOU ARE the devil!" I said in his direction. "You're both devils. Evil. I am but a pure and wonderful angel, sullied and beaten down by your wickedness." For some reason I had become all biblical and actually believed this to be true.

"Yes, Mum. You're an angel," Brendon sighed, "but an angel who needs some toast or something."

"Don't you feed me another goddam thing you poisonous…poisoner! You just went and bit the hand that feeds you. I fed you love and you fed me pain. I stopped for a minute thinking how poignant that was. "Where's my iPad? Have you taken it? Where is it? I need to make notes…"

Karl was just laughing his head off like a little kid. "Oh that's fucking hilarious."

"Why are you laughing?" I started to snicker too. At absolutely nothing and yet I was as tickled as a fat, drunk monk.

Karl was crying with happiness. Tears were running out of his eyes. His nose was running and his mouth was dribbling.

"Why is your face just continually leaking?" I asked with concern.

This just made him chuckle all the more. He was doubled over on the kitchen counter, head in hands, shaking with rapturous joy. I had never witnessed such a sight.

"Where's my iPad?" I asked out loud to no one in particular, as I wandered through to my study in search of it.

"Mum, I'm making you some toast!" Brendon shouted after me as I mooched aimlessly around.

"Go back from whence you came." I waved my arm at him as if to dismiss him from my space. "And say Hi to Beelzebub when you get there." I couldn't find my iPad anywhere.

The smell of hot buttered toast wafted in my direction and I suddenly felt quite peckish. "God, I am actually quite hungry."

Karl was already eating some and asking Brendon if he'd got any chocolate.

"I know Mum. It makes you starving. You'll probably want to eat loads."

"Starving? No. Not starving. You can't even comprehend starving." I picked up my toast and delighted in its buttery flavour. It tasted so much nicer than usual. After one and a half slices I'd had enough. That's when the epiphany hit me. "Wow! You know what?" I declared, putting down my half slice of toast, "nobody really needs two slices of toast, it's just greedy. One and a half is more than enough. If we ALL saved that other half instead of needlessly shoving it down our throats regardless, we could feed the world."

"The world?" said Brendon.

"Well yes, maybe – there's a lot of bread knocking around in houses you know!" I continued to gabble on, verbalising the stream of amazing thoughts that were washing through my monkey brain.

"I mean look at all the food we waste! We could take our leftovers and extra bits of stew and whatever and leave it in phone boxes!" I enthused.

"What the fuck?" Karl spat out his toast at the thought and began to laugh all over again.

"What the hell is wrong with you? I think you're possessed." I glared at him, starting to laugh myself. "Seriously, I've seen homeless people eating in phone boxes before. We should all take our food there. Buy extra and leave it inside the box. We could even bring back the iconic red phone boxes for this very purpose! Yes!

Marvellous. They could be the soup kitchens of the future!

"Mum that's the stupidest thing I've ever heard."

"There's no point in soup kitchens if you can't read," I stated.

"What?" said Karl, wiping the stream of steady tears from his face.

"If you can't read then you can't see that it says 'Soup Kitchen' can you. DUH. But everyone can see a red phone box. Even foreigners will understand that. People who have sought asylum here will even understand that. It's perfect!" I exclaimed in delight.

"What if they're colour blind?" Brendon asked.

"It's still a bloody phone box!" I retorted.

"But what if they're totally blind?" Karl giggled.

"Do you know what? This is just typical of your lack of creativity. You two with your cerebral brains, wanting to rain on my parade because you're incapable of thinking outside the box. Go to hell!"

"What box Mum? The phone box?"

I wandered through the house marvelling at how I was going to change the world. "Oh my God, it's brilliant! Where's my iPad?" I looked around hoping it would make itself visible. My astounding lucidity just HAD to be written.

CHAPTER 11

"Mum, I think you should chill out and sit down." Brendon followed me into my study as I went to look for my things.

"You BLOODY started this!" I began sifting through all the papers on my desk, desperately trying to find my Apple tablet." I need to get my thoughts into words…I'm having some *amazing* ideas."

"That's normal Mum, it makes you think. Everybody knows that."

"Well, you might know that and the people over there might know that and the people that…don't know *WHERE* they are might know that but…" I suddenly located my iPhone. That would have to suffice. Then I had another thought. "Where's my iPad Brendon? Did you sell it to furnish yourself with recreational drugs?" I peered into his eyes looking for any signs of lies like a trained profiler.

"Are you trying to 'out mentalist' me Mum?" He stared straight back at me. "You know that's impossible because I am *way* smarter than you."

"PFFT, you like to *think* that but I *actually* run rings

around you without you EVEN knowing. And if my iPad doesn't turn up I'll be selling your computer."

"Mum. Whatever. I thought you were weird before but you're actually fucking mental."

I took my phone and wandered in the direction of the happy buddha, Karl, who was giggling away on the sofa watching re-runs of Blackadder. I sat in the corner section of the settee and got to work.

MSG: TO COLIN FRAY: Hey Col, it's me Soph. Guess what – I've had an amazing idea about feeding people.

MSG: TO JOHN SMITH: Johnno, guess what, I think I could get Frank to sponsor an awesome idea I've had. Remind me on…that day I come to work.

I sat there waiting for them to reply. It took *forever* but in reality it was actually only two minutes. "Whoa, the time's on a go slow!" I said to Karl, "Everything seems to be taking *ages* but it's not really…Bizarre…"

"Sophie, the days are *always* long in this house." He smiled over at me. He was now looking completely relaxed and like he'd never, ever left us.

"Were you supposed to be going somewhere tonight?" I questioned, "you said not especially, when I asked earlier." My phone beeped." Hold on," I said, raising my hand to Karl to stop him responding.

COLIN FRAY: I know it's you Soph, it tells me it's you when you text ;) Feeding the people? What people?

SOPHIE RHODES: You know, the people…of the world. Well round here to start with but it could be a peno…pheromone…

"ARRR Fucking phone!" I said out loud to it as I texted.

Phenomenon! Seriously Colin, it's a new kinda soup kitchen idea!!!

Beep beep.

JOHN SMITH: You should be out enjoying yourself. We're all at the Canal House if you're interested.:P

SOPHIE RHODES: I can't – I've eaten cake. I'll see you in another life.

JOHN SMITH: What? LOL. Well, whatever it is, I can't wait to work with you on it :D

I put my phone down on the sofa and went off to find one of my many notebooks. I had a wonderful collection of them since I had a love of all things of paper and stationery. My adoration was so great that I couldn't bring myself to use some of them because they were too beautiful to spoil. I still felt as though I was walking on spongey ground and had to be very deliberate of my actions. I teetered slowly past Brendon, stationed at his Starship Enterprise.

"*Mommy!*" He leaned back in his chair and grabbed my arm.

"Don't touch me," I said, batting his arm away.

I found my books and decided life was too short to not use the damn things. Besides, now I had a drug lord in the house I may as well get writing in them before they got used at Rizla replacements. I picked out a stunning red leather one that had a long wrap around, leather cord to keep it closed. The paper pages were thick and lustrous; cream coloured and gilt edged. I lifted it to my nose and breathed in the rich scent of the new pages that were reminiscent of vanilla, talcum powder and beeswax polish. Ahhh...this one is perfect for such incredible ideas, I thought. I grabbed a pen and went back to the lounge of the Blackadder marathon. I sat back in my corner and opened my delightful book and ran my hand smoothly down the first page.

"What are you doing?" Karl looked over as his sleepy eyes broke away from Baldrick for a second.

"Changing the world," I replied, heady with belief. He smiled and returned to the TV.

I began to write: <u>Sophie's soup kitchens</u>. I underlined it as it was SO important.

Half slices of toast, bagged and saved.
leftovers from too much cooking.
leftovers collected from restaurants.
leftovers collected from peoples dinner parties.
Collections from Asda and Tesco before they shut shop.
Excuse to talk to that hot Greek bloke at the chippy.
Beautiful red phone boxes littering our land once more
and filled with people eating.
Maybe emergency blankets and cans of lager stored
inside.

My phone beeped.

COLIN FRAY: Don't we already have soup kitchens or something along those lines?

SOPHIE RHODES: Well I've never seen one – have you?

COLIN FRAY: Err, no, but I'm sure there's something.

SOPHIE RHODES: YES but not everywhere – I'm going to turn red phone boxes into a 'dining for one' experience!

COLIN FRAY: O…K…sounds peculiarly interesting. Better than the current conversation I'm having over here anyway!

SOPHIE RHODES: Are you in the canal with Johnno?

COLIN FRAY: You mean the Canal House?! No, I'm with Trudie and a selection of her friends in Tantra.

SOPHIE RHODES: A harem of women in Tantra bar! Tut tut, Colin. Maybe this one's a keeper then?! ;)

COLIN FRAY: It's £5 for a coke in here! Robbing bastards! And no, I'd rather be ANYWHERE else than here…sigh.

SOPHIE RHODES: A fiver for a coke! You can get a blow job for less than that in this city!

COLIN FRAY: SOPH!!

SOPHIE RHODES: I can't believe you haven't pulled rank and told the manager who you are! You can get free drinks like that you know…I do!

COLIN FRAY: Please tell me you DON'T do that..:O

SOPHIE RHODES: Only at McDonalds ;) Ok – I need to work on my phone boxes – go away and get busy with your bitches and I'll see you someday soon.

COLIN FRAY: Monday, Soph, Monday would be good. :D

Before I put down my phone I remembered 'The Voice.' I clicked on my game. I tried to play a remarkable word but couldn't seem to find one. I settled with AE on the side of something else. It was lame but it rid me of the irritable vowel syndrome.

SOPHISTICATION: So why are you called The Voice? What are you, a singer or something? A singing monkey perhaps?

I looked over at Karl who seemed to be in a world of his own, watching TV in a spaced out kind of way. I felt suddenly weary.

"Are you tired?" I asked.

"Very," he replied, laughing a little after he said it.

"What's so funny now?!" God, I'd never seen him laugh so much.

"We've been drugged by our son, and whilst I want to go crazy at him, I've actually been the most happy and relaxed than I have in a long time." He locked his eyes with mine and kept my gaze. I didn't like it and broke away. Way too uncomfortable. "It reminds me of the days when we used to have fun, when life was easy. Remember those days Soph?"

"Not nearly enough," I sighed. "They've been sullied by hardship and sadness."

"Look, let's go to bed," he suggested.

I looked at him blankly. Did he mean he was going to my bed? Wasn't he going to stay here on the sofa?

"Let me just sleep next to you. I want nothing else." He looked sincere and honest. "I just miss lying next to you and sleeping. Having someone warm nearby. Having *you* nearby." His eyes looked remarkably glossy but maybe I just wanted to see that. Besides, his face *had* been leaking all night long.

I sat in bed cloaked in my fluffy white dressing gown and propped up with pillows. I was scrolling through the e mails on my phone and though I was tired my mind was on fire. I also felt wildly uncomfortable about Karl sleeping in my bed. Our bed. Weird.

He came out of the en -suite dressed only in his Calvin Klein boxer shorts. I burst out laughing and looked away.

"What?" he smirked. "Have you forgotten what a fine looking specimen I am?"

"You're an arrogant wanker." I smiled. "This whole situation is insane. This whole *night* is insane." I mulled it over in my busy head.

He pulled back the sheets and got into the side of the bed where he once used to sleep like it was the most normal thing in the world. I moved my legs further to my side as he got in and felt myself stiffen.

"Ah, I love this bed."

I looked down at him as he grabbed his pillow and snuggled into it like a child. He glanced up at me, with a soft, dreamy expression. "Come and give me a cuddle, Soph."

I felt the familiar lurch in my stomach. A mixture of pain, longing and fear. It would be easy to fall into his arms and yield to the warmth and protection but it would be a short lived joy that would only serve to open up old wounds when the morning light fell on my face.

"In a bit.." I stalled. "I still have to change the world." I smiled and rubbed his hand under the sheets.

"You change everybody's world Sophie." He held onto my hand under the covers as he shut his eyes. "Don't be long," he whispered.

Please just go to sleep, go to sleep, go to sleep. I said the mantra over in my mind so I wouldn't succumb to him or to my own needs that were beginning to break through my protective wall.   I sat very still, holding onto his hand and watched him for several minutes as he drifted into dreamland.

I looked around the room and at the pretty Cath Kidston wallpaper that adorned the walls. It looked particularly shabby-chic in the soft glow of the bedside lamp. Faded flowers in pale, washed out blue. Shabby chic could pretty much sum me up of late, I thought wryly. I slipped my hand slowly out of Karl's. He was oblivious to the change and remained deeply unconscious. I still felt peculiar and wasn't sure if that was still the effect of the brownie or the surreal situation I was currently experiencing. I took my attention back to my phone and clicked on my word game. The Voice had played and my mood lifted a little.

THE VOICE: No I'm not a singing monkey. Sorry to disappoint.

I played my turn as I wondered why he had called himself 'The Voice.' User names tended to have some sort of relevance or aspiration attached to them.

> *SOPHISTICATION: OK. So are you a narrator? A politician? A pundit? A voice over person? Or maybe you just like the sound of your own voice…is that it?*

I waited for a reply. It was clearly wakey, wakey time in his part of the world. I must find out where that is, I thought. The little green bubble appeared along with his played word. It wasn't a great play and our scores were only a few points apart.

> *THE VOICE: No. I'm none of those things. Though I'm marveling at your sudden interest in me and the fact you are partaking in the art of conversation.*

> *SOPHISTICATION: Don't marvel too much. I'm just interested in people on the whole.*

But 'The Voice' was piquing my interest. I didn't know why and tried to analyse it. He was quite rude, *well*, maybe short and quippy rather than *really* rude. Besides, that didn't bother me. I lived in England where sarcasm and smart arses were usually the order of the day. He had certainly got under my skin in the first place which was always a sure fire way to get a reaction from me but it wasn't just that. Competitive, yes, he played the game well; intelligent and droll from what I could surmise at this early stage from his text and delivery. Challenging: almost certainly. These were attributes that I tended to like in a person.

THE VOICE: Oh and I thought it was just me. I'm almost hurt.

Hmm. I thought as I read his text. You are very droll indeed.

SOPHISTICATION: Almost? I must try a little harder in future.

The game was getting near to ending and I wondered if he'd just disappear back into the ether or we'd move on to round two.

THE VOICE: I work in the entertainment sector but I am nothing as glamorous as you imagine. What do you do? Something sophisticated?

I hated it when conversations took an about turn to focus on me. I didn't like talking about myself and my life. It seemed like an invasion of my privacy yet I was more than happy to do that to others. I always felt like I was expected to live up to something fabulous as my true reality would spark very little interest. I played my word and took the lead.

SOPHISTICATION: I write banal slot fillers for magazines.

That'll do, I thought.

THE VOICE: WOW. You sound like you really love your job.

SOPHISTICATION: I do like it, but on the whole that's what I do. Where do you come from Mr. Voice, another planet?

Maybe he'll leave 'the all about me' part alone now and I could direct the conversation back to him.

THE VOICE: I'd like to see some of your writing, if I may

Oh for the love of God. *Really?* Why? I wondered.

SOPHISTICATION: I really don't think you'd be interested it.

There. That should end that.

THE VOICE: How do you know whether I'd be interested in it or not? If I wasn't interested I wouldn't have asked.

SOPHISTICATION: Well, you really don't strike me as the sort of guy who'd rush home, kick off his shoes, lay on the sofa with a nice cappuccino as you hasten to read an article about the upcoming interior trends.

Only seven letters were left on my tile rack.

THE VOICE: I want to see your writing 'style'.

Style. Hmmm. Usually oppressed and lacking any spice or eloquence when you had to cram as much info about furniture and trend into a 300 word article. Still, he wasn't letting up so I sent a couple of links to the online magazines.

THE VOICE: Thank you. And I live in another planet called California.

Oh, it was like that was it? A quid pro quo.

So the voice was in Californ-I-A. That would explain the time difference. I tried to remember from my previous trips to San Fran and L.A – about 8 hours behind. Gorgeous, sunny days, palm trees and wide boulevards. He lived in the land of the beautiful where 'teeth, tits and toes' took priority. Well, not *all* of California, but that had been my initial reaction to LA LA land. I often wondered if one day ALL the women over there would carve, starve and Botox themselves into Stepford perfection; becoming similarly beautiful and yet so vacuous. And when that day came, the everyday, flawed and natural women from the other lands would dominate as the new beauties of the world as they stood uniquely next to the moulded.

SOPHISTICATION: Very nice. I'm jealous. Mostly of your sunshine and American bacon.

I finished my play and won by 11 points. I couldn't be certain but I was almost sure he'd allowed that to happen. The chat line remained open.

THE VOICE: Rematch, or does amusing and rare = one game stand?

I couldn't help but smile at his banter.

SOPHISTICATION: Of course. You may start one but I will resume 'rare and amusing' play tomorrow as I'm going to sleep, if that suits you?

THE VOICE: Tomorrow is fine. Going to bed means you live in Europe? England? France? Poland? Some island somewhere?

SOPHISTICATION: A remote island full of amusing monkeys. England.

THE VOICE: You have an isle of dogs, why not isle of monkeys. Sleep well English person.

Well he's either visited the East end of London or he's well read, I thought to myself. I scrolled back through our chat looking for meanings, and subtle shades; trying to build the character from across the pond in my mind and understand why I felt a connection with him.

I turned off my phone and let out a deep sigh. What a crazy world I lived in. I looked down at Karl who hadn't even moved and was sleeping soundly in another place. Just where I longed to be. I turned off the light and snuggled down into the bed so I too, could appreciate the nuance of an alternate reality like the deep sleeper beside me.

CHAPTER 12

I opened my eyes as the morning light flitted across my face from a gap in between the curtains. I felt Karl's arm draped heavy and warm across my waist. For a second my life felt safe and normal until the sudden wave of reality hit me like a sharp slap and caused me to physically gasp. I moved Karl's arm and jumped out of bed. I felt weak and uneasy and still in need of another eight hours.

"Jesus," I said out loud to myself. This is one screwed up family, I thought. Karl murmured and raised himself up on his elbow rubbing his forehead. He looked over at me and shook his head. Seemingly, the new dawn was hitting him in the same way.

"Oh fuck!" he suddenly exclaimed, sitting up with speed and looking for his phone at the side of the bed, "What time is it?"

I glanced down at my watch, "Eleven minutes past eight."

"Shit! I'm supposed to be in Brighton before 11." He started scrambling on the floor looking for last night's discarded clothes.

"Brighton? What for?" That was a good hour away

from Karl's work and where he had a flat but he was at least two hours away from Brighton here. And that was even if he drove at *his* speed.

"I've promised to help Sarah with her house hunting. She wants a place down there," he continued, bending over and pulling on his socks.

Sarah. Well what a surprise. Not.

Sarah was one of Karl's reps and though only twenty five years old and fourteen years his junior, she fawned over him like he was a potential sugar Daddy. On the few occasions I'd met her at Karl's Christmas work do's she had been barely able to even acknowledge me, which I found somewhat amusing. Everyone else at his company was a great crack and I'd usually end up in drunken debates with the European director and Jose, Karl's Spanish boss, until the early hours of the morning. The only time Sarah had paid me any attention was when she sat in the background intensely staring at me. Whilst she wasn't the prettiest of girls she had good body and made everyone fully aware of her passionate hobby of pole dancing *and* that her Facebook pictures were publicly available to anyone interested. That alone set her apart from her peers. Let's be honest, what red blooded male wouldn't while his days away wondering on the advantages of a girl who could remain upside down whilst doing the splits.

"Oh, the pole dancer. Why are you helping her?" I asked sarcastically, knowing this was a road I didn't really want to go down but being unable to help it anyway.

"She asked. I'm just being nice. And she's one of my

reps, not just a pole dancer." He looked up at me as if to make that point clearer somehow.

Of course he was being nice. That's what he did. What he'd always done. Mr. Saviour of all young and impressionable damsels. Nice and accommodating to *everyone else*.

"Is she sliding down the pole of your depravity?" I asked. I knew I was being a bitch but I couldn't help it. The near intimacy he'd dared to show me last night and now he was off on a junket with some exotic dancer. It pissed me off and made me feel stupid for even letting him sleep next to me.

"Really? Come on Soph, grow up."

I felt a sudden urge to smack him round the head. Lying sack of shit. It really wasn't any of my business but I resented the fact that he could go out and play whilst I was expected to deal with all the family stress every day. And I almost believed he missed me last night. I'm such an idiot.

Rather than carry on what would evolve into a futile argument, I removed myself from the room and went downstairs to get breakfast. The remains of last night's cake from hell lay over the kitchen counter which reminded me I'd got *that* to deal with too. I felt totally fed up and on the verge of becoming utterly atrocious. I knew I was going to have one of those days where I hated everything and everyone. The stall had been set and I could feel the vile darkness filling me up. Even if Santa Claus were to turn up in his red suit saying, "Hey, I'm for real!" I would probably tell him to fuck off.

I made a drink of tea and one for Karl despite not wanting to. He'd only find another reason to find me churlish if I didn't. I took mine into the living room and sat down. That's when I saw my beautiful red note book used and abused by my stupid ideas. I picked it up and read my notes. Though it was kind of ridiculous it was a fun idea. Then I recalled texting Colin and Johnno. I remembered telling my boss that he could get a blow job for a fiver. I groaned and put my head in my tea free hand.

Karl came into the room in his suit and looking *so* not Saturday morning. "Have you seen my car keys?"

"No. I've made you a drink. It's in the kitchen."

He went back through and I heard the jingle of his keys as he located them. He came back into the lounge. "Look, you need to have a serious word with Brendon about last night. I'm not going all out to support him at governors meetings if he's going to become a pot head. He needs a major attitude change all round."

"You think?" I retorted. "How about *YOU* have a word with him for a change instead of giving me a hard time about it and expecting me to deal with every.single.thing." I flicked my thumb through the corner pages of my newly abused notebook to try and distract myself from the rage building within.

"I don't have the time now, obviously. You do." He pulled his overcoat up from the back of the sofa where he'd left it last night and shrugged it on.

Yes Karl, I thought. I've got fuck all else to do. I hated him right now.

"Well so long as you've got your priorities straight." I gave my final dig.

"I'll talk to you another time," he replied flatly and walked out the front door. I heard his car rev up and drive away and I felt sick.

I sat with my tea and thought about my life: An ex husband who came and went as he pleased, solely fixed to his own agenda. A son I couldn't control, whom I had to battle with continually; a daughter who I had to ensure got tons of attention so she didn't feel left out. A job I was trying to hold down along with my 'flexible' hours so I could appease the school when Lord know-it-all, went off on one. A rambling house in need of constant upkeep; a garden full of ever growing plants; laundry, cleaning and cooking and not nearly enough money. Where was all this mentioned in the fairytales? I reckon Grimm wasn't even up to this nightmare. I was on stress out overload and I felt weak, lifeless and well ensconced on the wagon of self pity.

I lifted myself from the settee and stretched my whole body as high as I could. I'd read somewhere that if you fully stretched yourself out in the morning you'd get fifteen percent more energy. I had to get up and get on with it and 'carry-on-regardless' in true British style. I went around the house collecting pots and plates since nobody else understood how to do this. I looked at the remaining hash brownies and was stuck with a dilemma: Should I eat another and go back to the music of my mind, wrap them up and save them or chuck them away? I covered them with tin foil and hid them until I could decide. I spent the next few hours, cleaning, washing and scrubbing the house which in turn had the same affect on my mind; like clutter clearing of the soul.

My phone vibrated in my pocket.

BRYONY: Can you fetch me from Beth's in five minutes?

Ah. The taxi call. Another job to add to my curriculum vitae.

SOPHIE RHODES: Yes – be ready, I'm busy. X

I got in my car and drove through the family estates to fetch Bryony. She got in with a cheery smile. We had a chat about her night and then I went straight in for the kill to catch her off guard.

"How long have you known about Brendon doing weed?" I spotted her hesitation in a second.

"What?" she stumbled. "Is he?"

"Bryony. I know you know so let's cut the crap and start talking."

"Promise you won't tell him?"

"You have my word."

"Well, he used to *hate* it and call everyone that did it wasters. But then when he went to that party at Joe's house he tried some. He told me about it the next day and said it really made him feel good. I don't think he has it very often, just now and then.." She looked at me with wide eyes.

"And is it true that loads of teenagers are doing it?" I asked.

"Yes Mum. God, people do that more than they do *drinking*. People in the year below me do it. They meet down fag alley at the side of school at lunch or after and get high."

"God. *Really*?" I was shocked at this revelation. Hmm… that was one I could store up and use against Fothergill if I had to. Drugs at school in middle class suburbia.

"Have you ever had it?"

"No. No way Mum. I wouldn't even smoke!" I believed her but you never knew when the hand of temptation would come poking.

"Well that's good. But just so we're clear, If I EVER find out you have, then I will go ballistic. Totally. You understand?"

"YES! FINE. I get it."

"And don't get sucked into your brother's arguments that it's totally safe and harmless. It's an illegal drug for a reason. It messes you up. Trust me. He drugged me and Dad last night with cake and I went into magic roundabout land. Don't ever eat anything he gives you."

"LOL! You and Dad trippin' on weed! HA! That's joke!"

"No it's NOT. And don't give your brother *any* ammunition by saying so!" I pulled into the drive to see Brendon at the front door letting in four of his friends.

One of them was Luke. I got out of the car quickly and followed them in, giving Brendon a dirty look.

"How are you feeling Mommy?" Brendon said with a wicked grin.

"Annoyed. You'd be well advised to keep out of my way." I'd rather have sat him down and spoken to him alone but now all his friends were here that was going to have to wait until tomorrow. I said hello to his pals and then turned to Luke.

"Are you Catholic, Luke?" I asked lifting a rather nice rosary out from the mass of other gold chains he had draped round his neck. Luke was the epitome of Chavtastic and so wildly different from Brendon's other friends. I never saw him without a snapback, tracksuit, a different pair of trainers nowadays referred to as 'fresh creps' and some sparkly earring in his pierced ear.

"Err, no. I'm not Catholic. I don't believe in God," he answered looking a little perturbed.

"Oh well that's a good thing," I retorted, letting the dark rosary beads fall from my hand, "or you'd be doing a lot of Hail Mary's tomorrow for your sins," I smiled.

"What sins?"

"The hash brownies?" I offered. "Did your Mum and Dad enjoy them too?" He looked at me sheepishly and at a loss for words.

"Mum, leave him alone and stop being such a *fucking* bitch!" Brendon's friends all looked to the floor, embarrassed by him swearing at me and the whole awkwardness of the situation.

"Watch your mouth." I walked away to the utility room. I knew that it wasn't Luke's fault I'd been fed hash brownies but I wanted him to know I wasn't happy. He was involved, after all.

I turned on the iron and looked at the piles and piles of clothes waiting to be pressed. 'Sham, drudgery and broken dreams' the line from the Desiderata poem hanging on the utility wall jumped out at me as the iron hissed to life in my hand. Now my clean house was full of teenage boys who would no doubt, just make it messy again. I pulled a t-shirt from the pile and flattened it out on the ironing board, making a start on my Saturday afternoon's entertainment.

I'm probably the only person on the planet who looks forward to Mondays, I thought.

My weekends were a succession of patience, persistence and perspiration with what seemed like very little reward. The daytime of domesticity rolled into evening and hoards of teenagers ran amok in my space. I went to the living room and shut the door to hide away the raucous behaviour that was aggravating my spirit. Oh for one day of peace. Just one.

My friend Lisa kept texting me, insisting that I come to her party but I continued refusing with various excuses. I just couldn't face getting trussed up and having to pretend to *like* people, particularly since she had said there was someone going she'd like me to meet and had told them all about me. Ugh. No. That would mean I'd have to be super pleasant and charming as well as go steady on the wine. Where was the fun it that?

"But you'll really like him. He's gorgeous and witty and everything you like!" she enthused. "And I just KNOW he'll *love* you."

Pressure. No thanks. Every day living was enough for me right now without taking on the possible awkward, first steps of romance.

Earlier, when I'd made it half way through the ironing pile, Brendon had thrown a DVD over to me saying, "Here, watch this. Now *there's* a drug that should be invented." Before I could react, he'd then chucked an opened packet of chocolates at me with one remaining, sweaty sweet: the last one in a tube of Rolo's. Despite being annoyed with him I'd had to smile. Ever since being a little boy he'd always saved me his last chocolate because the Nestle advert on the telly had said, *"Do you love anyone enough to give them your last Rolo?"* I found it heart warming that he still did it, like it was a lifelong tradition.

I spent the following two hours on the sofa with my iPad reading the links that he'd sent me about the benefits of marijuana. I had to admit that I found the 'Amazing Atheist' an entertaining chap. I then sourced my own information on the long term, nasty side effects that I emailed back to him. I could not get into a discussion with Brendon unless I'd gone through everything on both sides of the argument or he wouldn't even entertain it. Not that he was likely to listen anyway.

After I'd finished my extensive research I clicked on

word and saw that 'The Voice' had started a new game as promised. Round two. I smiled. I accepted the request and saw that he'd placed a seven letter word and got himself a bingo to boot scoring seventy points. I hated it when that happened because it meant that you were way behind before you'd even started. Not that it mattered in this case. Whilst I still wanted a good game, the play here had become more about the chat bubbles than the score.

> THE VOICE: *I think this game might be more challenging for you than the last.*

I didn't doubt it. And on more than one level. I played a reasonable 20 pointer.

> SOPHISTICATION: *You have a fair chance of winning but it is early days, my friend.*

I decided I'd look at the film that Brendon had thrown in my direction. Limitless. Hmm. A bit like my patience. I read the back of the DVD cover: *'A writer discovers a top secret drug which bestows him with super human abilities.'* Starring Bradley cooper, Robert De Niro and and Abbie Cornish. Yes. That did sound like an interesting drug. I could sure use some super human abilities right about now. I put the film in the DVD player and settled down to watch it. Escaping to another world for a few hours was just what I needed and I was definitely up for taking some NZT-48 by the time the film finished.

I clicked on my game before I made my way to bed.

THE VOICE: So now I've notched up a level, from amusing monkey to friend?

SOPHISTICATION: Well, let's just see how it goes shall we?

THE VOICE: How was your evening?

SOPHISTICATION: I'm watching a film. Correction. I watched a film.

THE VOICE: Which movie?

SOPHISTICATION: Limitless.

THE VOICE: Now I'm jealous of Bradley Cooper.

Bradley Cooper was the main character who played the drug taking writer. By usual standards he would make it to any woman's 'Top twenty, shaggable celebrity list', but not mine. And 'The Voice' was jealous of him? An interesting development and one that made me catch my breath a little.

SOPHISTICATION: You've no need to be. Besides, I prefer Robert De Niro.

THE VOICE: Now I'm jealous of De Niro.

Wow. Where was *this* going, I wondered. We seemed to be moving swiftly from banter to flanter and Mr. California was certainly getting into my head, that's for sure.

I went to bed emotionally drained. As I snuggled down I recognised the faint smell of Karl's cologne from where he'd slept the previous night. I wondered whether he was doing the horizontal tango with his dancing friend and felt upset and pissed off at the same time. I turned over and shut my eyes begging sleep to take me away from this hell of a life. I drifted on and off in fits, primarily because I had a stream of teenagers running up and down the stairs, shouting and laughing and totally oblivious to the needs of the sleeping. I could hear the distant tones of both Ed Sheeran and Taylor Swift playing from different areas of the house. Doors were banging and creaking; taps were being open and closed along with clinking glasses and plates. I wanted to go downstairs and either shout or join in but I was physically and mentally wasted. Part of me didn't want to spoil their joy either because the fun and freedom of youth is such a short lived experience. I decided to text:

MSG: TO BRYONY, BRENDON: Can you keep it down – I'm trying to sleep.

BRYONY: Yeah..Soz x

BRENDON: K, famalam. Love you xx

I lay in bed in the dark wondering if life was *ever* going to be any different for me as I listened to the haunting Ed Sheeran lyrics permeating my door, *"Lights gone, day's end, struggling to pay rent, long nights, strange men.."*

CHAPTER 13

Sunday morning came with relentless, pounding rain. I hated the rain, it always put me on a downer. I passed Brendon's room and peered through one of the empty squares where there had once been glass. He'd slammed his door so hard in temper one day, that it had completely smashed and I didn't see the point of replacing it for him to do it again. All bar one of last night's friends lay in lumps around his room. It stank of teenage sweat, overused clothes and something I couldn't decipher. Disgusting. I hurried downstairs in case it permeated my clothes.

My house was wrecked: Pizza boxes, muddy trainers, cups, glasses and empty crisp packets lay all around. I felt like waking them all up like a screaming banshee and forcing them to clean it up but it was just easier to do it myself. The rest of the morning carried on in the same vein, as was the norm.

Afternoon soon arrived and Brendon and his friends slowly emerged downstairs complete with their living stench, like Pig-Pen from Peanuts. They mooched around filling bowls with colossal amounts of Cheerio's and Coco Pops; enough to feed a village.

"*Mommy*," Brendon said grabbing hold of me in a bear hug and not letting me go. "You're awesome sauce." He squeezed me tight and lifted me up high off the floor.

"ARRR put me down! I have a weapon and I'm not afraid to use it." I pointed the potato peeler at him.

"Got myself a chick last night Mama!" he said, flexing his muscles and making his friends spit their Cheerios all over my table.

"Oh..?"

"Yep. She's been after me for months but..you know, I let her sweat for a bit."

"You're such a dick Brendon," Joe sniggered, "you know she's only going out with you so she can get close to me."

"Yeah whatever, Joe, you fag." He walked over to Joe and put him in a friendly headlock as he tried to eat his cereal.

"And who is this girl?" I asked.

"Her name, *Mother*, is Jessie."

"You mean Hussy," Tom chipped in from the table.

"Shut the *fuck* up Tom, you waste man. *Like man won't leng you down!* Brendon joked. "When you're as hench as me then the babez may come a running...but... that's never going to happen to you, *fat* boy!"

I found it amusing that boys used insults as a term of endearment. Especially Brendon. He would always take it one step further than most, picking out all their faults and weaknesses and using them as ammunition. I wondered how his friends coped with him sometimes. They either found him fun and refreshing or were too scared to make a fuss.

"I hope she ISN'T a hussy!" I said. The last thing I needed was some young girl being knocked up, "And how old is she?"

"Sixteen and sweet." He smiled at his mates who all cracked up laughing. "No seriously Mum, she's really nice. The only problem is she's a devout Catholic. You know what I'm sayin'.."

"Well good. I'm glad she is. Maybe she can teach you some morals and how to be pleasant. Maybe she'll convert you into a good boy since I am unable to get through to you."

"ERRR – not gonna happen *Mommy*. I am a true atheist. God is for people who are just scared of dying."

I left the God conversation for now. I'd been in that debate several times and told Brendon that he shouldn't argue with people who had faith in something just because he thought it was a load of bullshit. I was glad he'd met a nice girl and just hoped he wouldn't start trying to argue with her about religion. I also hoped she'd last longer than the other girls before her who had been instantly discarded when they got too needy.

His friends finished their breakfast and got ready to leave so they could all get back together virtually in the next hour, to fight the bad boss. As I shut the door to them and said goodbye I was left in the hallway with Brendon.

"I'm going for a shower." He went to go upstairs.

"Wait! " I demanded, "I want to talk to you. I want to

go through this issue with marijuana. I'm really not happy about it and what you did to me and your Dad. And the governors meeting. We need to discuss that. You need to start behaving. Big time."

"Not now, I'm too tired. Look, the weed thing, get over it. I'm going to have it now and then so I can either *tell* you about it or do it behind your back. Make a choice. I know I've got to try harder at school. I GET IT Mum. You don't have to keep going on about the same shit."

"Well I'm not supporting you any more unless you make a massive effort."

"Yeah, Mum. Yes you will. And I do make an effort, believe it or not. "He trudged upstairs indicating that the conversation was now over.

I let it go. Picking your moments was crucial in order to stop a kick off. Sometimes you just had to trickle your concerns through via constant nagging and pray he eventually got the message.

I went to the living room and flicked on the magic box. There was nothing particularly interesting on. I hated Sunday nights. They always seemed a little depressing and uncomfortable like that night before school feeling. I turned, as always, to my virtual entertainment and to 'The Voice'. God. I was miles behind score wise.

SOPHISTICATION: I like his acting skills. That's all.

I got sidetracked by the TV for a second. A woman on the Antiques Road Show had just brought in a little flowery vase she'd purchased at a car boot sale and found out it was worth thousands. I must take a look round this house, I mused. Money was getting so tight lately.

I checked the game.

THE VOICE: May I see a picture of you?

I re-read the message several times. Here we go. Just when I thought you had a bit more about you Mr. Voice.

I'd met these sorts before on games. Normally they were straight in there with the "Got any saucy photos?" Yeah mate, because of *course* I'm gonna send you a picture of my tits so you can wank yourself stupid over them. *Really*? I'd usually reply with, "I'm a transvestite. Do you want me normal or in drag?"

Another message appeared.

THE VOICE: I just mean a normal picture. Of your face. Nothing pervy. If you're not comfortable with it that's absolutely fine.

Now he'd put it like that it seemed perfectly acceptable. However, I was still nervous. I felt like I was on a back to front date and I didn't know how it had got to this point without me realising.

SOPHISTICATION: OK then. If you insist. How shall I get it to California?

The Voice sent me an email address via the chat message bubble. For some reason, getting an email address seemed serious.

I wondered what picture to send and whether I really wanted to go down this road. I scrolled through my iPad looking through my camera roll at the collection of photographs. 'No, I don't like that one – my hair's too messy, absolutely no sign of sophistication there. Hmm, look a bit hammered on that one…no, no, not the Halloween one in my pussy cat suit…Oh my God, whatever possessed me to buy that shirt..eww. And on it went. Finding a normal picture amongst my photos was proving more difficult than I thought. And why did I care? Why was it important that I was visually pleasing to this man in the ether? But for some reason, it was.

Eventually I opted for my FB profile picture. Smiling face shot, outside of work with my sunglasses on. Normal. I pressed send and heard the email sound *whoosh* it off across the Atlantic. I sat still looking at my iPad not knowing what to do next and feeling anxious. I felt like a stupid teenager and inwardly chastised myself. I closed my tablet and went to make a cup of tea. I then washed the pots and cleaned down the kitchen surfaces and then made a shopping list. Anything to bring back the feeling of normalcy.

I returned to the sofa with my cuppa and stared at my closed tablet, not daring to open it but dying to at the same time. I had two messages: One on my email and one on my game. I opened the e mail message first.

A smiley face. *A smiley face? That was it?* I hated emoticons. Particularly on their own as they were too ambiguous. I only used them myself to appease others. I'd had my texts misconstrued on many an occasion and therefore had to add them at the end of everything I sent, along with kisses so people didn't read it in the wrong way and get upset with me. Annoying.

But what did a smiley face mean on its own? I like it? Thanks? I can't really be arsed to respond? Actually, not as attractive as I was expecting?

I moved swiftly on to the chat bubble message.

> *THE VOICE: Thank you but I need another. Without sunglasses. I want to see your eyes.*

Wow. For some reason that *really* moved me. He wanted to see my eyes. It was soft and chivalrous and the idea of him looking into the windows of my soul had a certain quixotic appeal. I sat there for a moment wondering what to do. I felt like I'd walked into a situation that I didn't understand or a conversation I wasn't part of. I was at odds with myself. *Why* did I have to analyse everything to death, I thought. It's just a photo. Of my eyes. No big deal.

I scrolled through the pictures again trying not to be

so picky and found one. I sent it before I had time to change my mind. Again I sat there, still, waiting for whatever was going to happen next.

I didn't get a smiley face back. I didn't even get a return mail. I just got a message in the game in the little green chat bubble.

THE VOICE: It's perfect.

CHAPTER 14

I was always knackered on a Monday morning. I'd open my eyes at the sound of the alarm and feel nauseous with fatigue. Except that never happened at the weekend, oh no. My eyes would ping open and my brain would be saying, *"Come on, get up, lots to do, come on, let's go."* On a Monday it wasn't even responsive.

I crawled out of bed and thought about how I was going to explain my drug induced behaviour to my boss. Ugh.

The calendar on my phone beeped on my dressing table reminding me it was Brendon's paediatrician appointment. We had to go as they usually liaised well with the school on what he needed support wise. Not that anything ever changed. I'd forgotten on Friday to ask Colin if this was OK. *Damn.* I was sure he'd be alright with it but I knew I was taking the rise with my flexible hours at work. I got ready quickly and woke Brendon up telling him we had an appointment with Kathy.

"Oh for fucks sake. I don't want to go. Can I have the rest of the day off school after?"

"No. You've got exams this year, so no," I reiterated.

"I can pass them in my sleep."

"Just get up! You said you'd try so how about sticking to that and getting up. NOW!"

I went downstairs to ring Colin. He answered in seconds.

"Hi Colin, It's me Sophie."

"Yes, Soph, I KNOW it's you, your name comes up when you ring."

"Oh yeah, I don't know why I do that..Anyway, I forgot about an appointment at Brendon's paediatrician this morning. I have to go which means I'll be in late..is that OK?" God, I felt really bad about doing this.

"Yeah, sure but it means you'll miss this morning's meeting."

I clasped my hands over my eyes and sighed. I'd forgotten that too.

"But we can go through it when you get in. What time will that be?"

"About ten -ish…" I offered tentatively.

"Ok babe. See you then and you can tell me all about the phone box idea!"

I suppressed a groan and said my goodbye's quickly.

After dropping Bryony at school, Brendon sat very quietly in the car staring straight ahead.

"Are you alright?" I inquired. He seemed very subdued, which was odd. Nice, but odd.

"Tired."

I decided to take the opportunity to talk to him, since he was in a calm frame of mind and stuck next to me in the car, unable to escape.

"You know what I said yesterday? You know, about behaviour.." I gave him a sideways glance as I drove and he remained fixated to the road ahead. "It's really important that you reign in a little. Try not to react to teachers if they something you don't like." I looked over as we stopped at the traffic lights. He was still staring straight ahead like he was in a trance. "It's really important that we get through your exams and th.."

Suddenly, he lurched forward and punched the dashboard again and again. I froze in the seat, flabbergasted and expecting the passenger airbag to explode at any minute. The car behind tooted me because I was oblivious to the lights turning green. I drove forward slowly trying to find a place to pull up.

"Just shut the FUCK UP," he yelled. "Stop the fucking car." He opened the glove compartment and slammed it shut. He then moved his hand onto the handbrake. "Stop the fucking car or I WILL."

I pulled over quickly onto the zig-zags outside a primary school where I wasn't supposed to. A woman walking by and pushing a buggy gave me a dirty look, like I was a stupid parent who thought she could just stop where she wanted and flaunt the rules.

"Brendon.." I didn't know what to do. My heart was pounding. Where had this rage come from?

"Stop fucking talking," he shouted. I stopped and remained quiet, wondering how to deal with this. He yanked off his seat belt and opened the car window wide. His breathing was laboured. Leaning suddenly forward in the seat, he clasped his hands behind his neck and bent his head down to his knees. After several minutes, he then sat up, opened the car door and got out, slamming it hard behind him.

"Where are you going?" I called after him. He didn't answer. I watched as he paced up and down the street, tight faced and angry. I saw him taking deep breaths and stretching his arms up high and gripping his hands tightly together. My heart was racing and I felt powerless. I could normally see when he was going to flip out but I hadn't seen that coming.

A man in his late forties with three kids in tow stopped at the open, passenger side window and leant down to speak to me. "You can't park here love – zig zags." He waved his arms at the connecting yellow 'V's painted on the floor. "Have you passed your test?"

"I'm sorry…really sorry… I know. I had to stop because my son was unwell." I replied, feeling like crying and pulling at a piece of thread on my skirt.

"Well you coulda drove down a few more yards, this *is* a school, it's dangerous." He walked off chuntering about me as he made his way to the school gates. A lot less dangerous than my son yanking up the handbrake and causing a serious accident near children, I thought. But he hadn't seen that part. *He,* like the woman in the buggy, just assumed I was some dilatory Mother, with no regard for anyone as was always the case. It made me hate people.

Brendon came back to the car and got in. "Just drive," he said, "let's get this shit appointment over."

I pulled away from the kerb and kept quiet. We had to get to the paediatrician and I needed him to be calm. He'd tell me what all that was about when he was ready. We parked up at the back of the health centre and made our way to reception. The centre was having a refurb and we were directed to a different corridor than usual to sit and wait. The hallway was quite dim and had three wooden doors to different clinics. We sat down on the waiting chairs and I grabbed an old magazine and started going through it; trying to distract myself from the nausea inside. Brendon sat next to me looking at the pictures as I flicked through.

"She's such a slag," he remarked, as a picture of Jordan came to view.

"She's actually very clever at what she does," I answered, glad that he was now entering into conversation with me and finding equilibrium.

"I hate girls who look like her. She's a tart."

I ignored the comment and carried on reading the wasteful gossip as we waited for Kathy to become available. Suddenly Brendon got to his feet, arms folded and clearly agitated. I looked up quickly, praying he wasn't about to lose it again.

"Come on," he urged, "there's no fucking way I'm going in there." He nodded his head back to one of the closed doors.

"What? Why? What's the matter Brendon?"

"Err… have you seen what it says on the door? This place is *freaky* man. Come on!"

I looked at the plaques on the door wondering what the hell he was on about. "What *are* you talking about?"

"The door…DUH…Have you *read* what is says," he pointed at the door plaque, "*PHYSIO THE RAPIST*"

I leaned back in my chair and laughed out loud, letting the magazine slide from my lap. That was priceless. I'd never known anyone that could take me from absolute despair to raucous laughter in the space of a few minutes like Brendon could. "It's *physiotherapist*," I said. "As in fiz-ee-oh-therapist." I was still chuckling at how he'd read it and loving the naivety of his mind despite how intelligent he was. "It's a name for a person that helps with physical therapy and movement..that sort of thing."

"Well it's retarded and I'm not going in that room." He remained standing, arms crossed, whilst we waited for Kathy.

The appointment went by fairly quickly, mostly due to Brendon being as difficult as possible. I didn't mind that too much because at least she got to see what he was like to deal with and would report this back to the school in a favourable way for Brendon. We went through some of his behaviour at school of late including the fact he'd upped onto governors report and so on. I wanted to mention taking weed but I'd have to do that when alone with her otherwise he would go ballistic. He wasn't responding well to being questioned this morning and had burst out with a "Why does everyone keep talking and telling? Why don't they shut the hell up and start listening?" Ah, so that's what the rage had been about. I felt for him. I knew it was difficult but only he could find a way to manage his emotions.

We left with an 'open appointment' as Brendon had said he didn't see the point in constantly discussing his condition with people that had never experienced it themselves.

We drove back to school in silence as I didn't want to overload him. I didn't dare say *"behave yourself"* as I think that would have just tipped him over the edge. I wished him a good day as he left the car.

I got to work at 10.15am and went straight through to see Colin. I noticed Johnno wasn't there as I passed his desk.

"Thanks Colin. Sorry about all this flexi – time," I apologised as I removed my jacket, "what did I miss?" I sat in his leather chair as he talked me through the mornings meeting and what he wanted me to cover.

"There's an invite to World Service in a few weeks, I've put you and I down as attending…if that's alright?" He was going through his blackberry looking for the date.

"Yeah, sure.." World Service was a really exclusive restaurant so I felt honoured that Colin had asked me to go along with him.

"So – what's this phone box idea then Soph?" He looked up with a big smile.

"Oh God. I'm so sorry about that. You won't believe what happened. Brendon fed me hash brownies and I went cuckoo. Just ignore EVERYTHING I said." I blushed a little, now I was having to explain myself.

"HA HA! That's hilarious. I like his style. How did the meeting go?"

"Well, Karl came and managed to save the day for once and basically told them they were shoddy and unprepared with a severe lack of understanding and procedure. He bought us some time and hopefully I can get him through his exams before he gets himself expelled. " I twiddled with the pen in my fingers, "Thanks Colin, you really are good to me and I *really* do appreciate it."

"No worries babe." He looked so sincere but then he did have those kind of blue eyes that did that.

"Where's Johnno by the way, is he out on something?"

"He's got a groin injury from a charity five a side yesterday. Says he's in agony!" Colin shook his head.

I left his office and went to my desk. I was so going to rib Johnno about that. I got my phone out to text him.

MSG: TO JOHN SMITH; Aww poor baby…does it hurt?

My phone rang before I could put it down saying Hillfields School. No. No way. Surely he can't have done something wrong already; in *just* two hours. I took in a deep breath and answered.

"Hi Sophie, It's Janice."

"Please tell me he hasn't kicked off already…"

"Err no, actually he hasn't but if you can come in sometime later or tomorrow then I need to see you."

"Oh? Well I'll have to check with my boss. It's

probably going to have to be tomorrow first thing, if I can. What's the problem?"

"Mr. Fothergill had to change all his arrangements this morning. The school had an impromptu visit from Victor Churchman in respect of something that Brendon has done."

"What?" Oh. My. God. Victor Churchman, the Labour MP has visited the school because of Brendon. The enormity of it ran through my mind.

What the hell had he done now?

I sat at my desk looking at my phone and wondering whether or not to ring Karl. Should I tell him that MP's were now coming into school because of our son or should I wait to see what it was all about first? Probably better. He'd only irritate me and I wanted a bit more time to lapse between us from after the brownie incident. I couldn't possibly go to school this afternoon because I'd already rolled in late but being late again tomorrow was just royally taking the piss. I put my phone down and went to Colin's office. He was on the phone but beckoned me in to take a seat until he'd finished.

"Colin, I need to take a few days holiday," I said quickly.

"Oh? Late deal or something?"

"I wish! When do I ever go on holiday, Colin?" I laughed. However it wasn't funny. I could die for a break somewhere in Europe. The sun glistening on the blue

Mediterranean; flip flops and floaty frocks; long glasses of sangria and lazing by the pool. I couldn't afford such luxuries and I wouldn't leave Brendon with anyone else and he would not go on holiday unless it involved sport and snow. My time off was usually spent decorating, gardening and catching up with the ironing.

"I need to go into school again. Apparently Victor Churchman has been in regarding Brendon."

"Victor Churchman? What the hell for?" Colin looked quite surprised.

"I've no idea. They will only tell me when I get there. It's Mr. Fothergill's way of asserting control, like I'm one of his pupils or something. I was thinking about going tomorrow which is why I need to take a few days. I'll still work at home but I'd rather take it as holiday."

"Just go, it's not a problem."

"No Colin. It is a problem. It's very good of you to be so accommodating but it's not fair to everyone else. It makes me feel bad and like I'm getting preferential treatment. That's going to cause resentment sooner or later."

"Everyone knows how hard you work Soph," he sat with his chin resting on his hand looking at me as though trying to figure me out, "it's only a phase and you get your work done, so I don't mind." He gave a hopeful smile.

"But Aspergers *isn't* a phase. I need to get him sorted out Colin and I'd rather take it as holiday but still work in-between to make up for my time off. *Please*?", I begged.

"How long?"

"Maybe three days, starting tomorrow?"

"OK – It's yours."

"You're the best Ed in the world." I grinned at him as I stood up to leave. He sat back in his chair smiling as he watched me leave.

I got my head down for the rest of the day which was a lot easier without Johnno there until I received a text back from him.

JOHN SMITH: I'm in severe pain Soph, but scored a hat trick! Better than Frank.

SOPHIE RHODES: You're not even in Frank's league Johnno – He's premiership material. Plus he wouldn't be wussing about a little groin strain!

JOHN SMITH: I bet you're missing me!

SOPHIE RHODES: How can I miss you when you won't stop texting me. Go away. I'm busy.

I actually *was* missing Johnno but I'd never tell him that. It was nice to have a bit of banter whilst you worked and he was so easy to reel in.

The day passed quickly and I managed to get a ton of articles sorted which made me feel like I'd made up for my poor attendance. I arrived home about 6.30pm to find Bryony, Brendon and 'new girlfriend' at the Starship Enterprise watching YouTube videos. I'd wanted to talk to him about the 'MP' coming in and get the heads up on what he'd done. However, when I'd rang Janice Armitage earlier to make an appointment she'd asked me not to so we could all go through it together. I hated being on the back foot.

Brendon came through to the kitchen with his new chick. "This is Jessie, Mother," he announced as he put his arm round her neck.

"Hi Jessie," I enthused, "lovely to meet you and I *love* that scarf you're wearing." I picked up the delicate turquoise material around her neck that was imprinted with multicoloured butterflies.

"Oh, you too! And thank you," she smiled, "it's from Top Shop."

I loved her instantly: Well spoken, friendly and pretty to boot.

Brendon remained on his best behaviour all night and even sat at the table for dinner because Jessie made him. Who'd have thought that all we'd ever needed was a nice girl to sort him out.

CHAPTER 15

The following morning I let Brendon and Bryony walk to school together whilst I did a bit of work from home. My appointment with school wasn't until 10.am and they wanted to see me on my own first. I hadn't said a word to Brendon about coming in, just like they had asked.

I arrived at reception and Janice was already downstairs waiting to meet me. We went up to her office and sat down.

"Right," she said, as she removed a piece of paper from a file, "this is what's happened. Apparently Brendon is unhappy with the way the IT department is being run and so a few weeks back, he took it upon himself to write an email to Victor Churchman. Quite frankly, *I think* it's a very well written letter for his age but it is Brendon we are talking about! Mr. Fothergill is slightly upset as we had an impromptu visit from Victor who is now looking into the school system." She handed over the printed e mail for me to read:

From: *BRENDON RHODES*
To: *CHURCHMAN, VICTOR*
Subject: Hillfields School Improvements.

Dear Victor

I am a pupil at Hillfields School and I would like to address a few issues with you seeing as you are our MP.

Firstly, I have no big problem with the school. I've learnt a lot in the past few years, not just from an intellectual point of view but also socially. However, there are a few things bugging me that I think you may be able to help with.

Well, first off I think the technology is very, very behind- this includes all Adobe products (around 5-6 years behind) and the computers are even further back than that. Seeing as this school is a technology college I find it incredibly annoying and frustrating that we don't have, I hesitate to say a new…but at least up to date technology. Adobe CS6 has been launched and I have tried and tested it myself at home, the school has Adobe CS3, which, as I said, is half a decade behind. What's the use of teaching someone to edit in Photoshop CS3 when there's a different, easier way in CS6. This will negatively impact the jobs of pupils in the future when they've only learnt about CS3. This happens with all programs in school associated with Adobe. Another thing is, in my information Technology class, we've been learning to create websites in Dreamweaver CS3. I was very excited to help out my class mates because I learnt about this at home (mostly because I was so interested, I finally began to create sites for my family with up to date methods) And when it came to the lesson, the teacher started to teach them how to work with tables. You might not know, but if you go to any website in the entire world you'll only see them made with CSS, which is a programming language, easy enough to learn, in Dreamweaver. I was extremely disappointed finding out that the school were teaching people wrongly so I told the teacher that he should show the class how to make websites using div tags and CSS. His reply was, "What are those?"

If you haven't got my point already, then I'll put it clearer. This school has many people that would like to work in the IT department. It's one of the reasons I chose this school from others and I'm extremely disappointed finding out that all the years I've been here that I've been taught the most out of date methods ever. If there's anything you can do I'd be extremely appreciative. I realize it's not the schools fault that they haven't got the budget but I think you could remedy that situation. I have even made a tutorial on how to create websites using CSS and div tags and sent it to the entire class year. This hasn't made a significant impact but at least I'm trying eh?

They may not have the biggest budget what with the 6th form center being burnt down and money being invested in other places, but the whole of CS6 – which would drastically improve learning and success rates- is only £800.00. They could pay this onetime fee and install it on their servers during a half term and it would be ready for everyone to learn to use. If they have problems with CS6, which I don't think they will, why not get CS5? They're neglecting the schools IT department and whilst most other schools won't have it, THIS school is based on technology and I don't see any reason not to pay £800.00.

Don't think of it as a program but as something that would increase learning to those interested in IT, designing, etc,- by 10 fold – CS6. Maybe also update their computers, though this is not a necessity because of the massive costs.

I really do hope you can help and I'll thank you in advance for just giving your time to read this letter/ email.

Regards, Brendon Rhodes.

As I read the letter in front of Janice I couldn't help but snigger at some of the things he'd said and I was quite impressed at the composition of the e mail.

"It's pretty good, actually," I said to Janice.

"Yes, it is, *very* well formulated, in fact."

"So, what exactly happened then, with Victor Churchman and Mr. Fothergill?"

"Well, the problem is, Mr. Fothergill feels that if Brendon had issues with the school he should have come to senior staff or himself first. Involving politicians makes problems for him if they think the school is being run inefficiently."

Yes, I thought. I bet he didn't like that one bit. He was all about the SAT's results and exam passes and becoming the leading school in the area. Now Brendon had made his technology college look like a joke. Particularly since the IT teacher didn't even understand the methods that Brendon had suggested.

"Oh. So how does this affect him on governors report? Is this like another black mark against him?"

"I suppose it depends on the outcome," she raised an eyebrow. "Mr. Fothergill is none too pleased but it would depend on how the governors feel. However, I have to discuss more on that since last week's meeting."

Ah, the result of the governors meeting. I waited for her to tell me how that had been received after we'd left. I didn't feel on so much of a high now.

"After discussing it with Mr. Fothergill, Mr. Locks has decided that we need to put Brendon on an individual timetable plan and perhaps remove him from one or two lessons. Just concentrate on his ten key exams and then have him leave school."

"Leave school? What do you mean *leave* school?" I started to panic.

"Basically just come in when he needs to for the relevant lessons and then go home. We believe that this is the only way to keep him from being in any more trouble than necessary and from risking expulsion."

"What do you mean, remove him from other lessons?" I wondered where this was going.

"Well there was an incident in Business Studies that we've yet to talk about." She flicked, as usual, through the reports.

My mouth went dry and I forgot to breathe. All of a sudden the school had made all these monumental decisions in the space of two days.

She read out the incident:

Mr. Jenkins – Business studies – Brendon kept asking me to explain a part of the business sector as he said he wanted more information. I asked him to refer to the text book in front of him. Brendon continued to ask me to elaborate stating that the text book was not 'in depth' enough and he wanted me to explain certain modules. I told Brendon that this was all we needed to cover for today's lesson and all the relevant information pertaining to that was in the text book. Brendon said "You're obviously refusing to explain this to me as you don't understand business properly. Your job as my teacher is to explain all the concepts." I told Brendon that my job was to stick to the lesson plan to ensure all pupils covered the exam criteria. Brendon then replied with, "Well, if you understood business properly then you'd be running one and wouldn't be a teacher on £25K a year". I found Brendon's remarks rude and unnecessary and asked him to leave the lesson.

I winced at his comment to the teacher and couldn't believe he'd had the gall to say something like that. "Oh no… Why can't he just keep his mouth shut?" I shook my head at Janice.

"Look," she said, "it's part of the way he thinks but we need to keep him in line. The idea of this plan is that he sticks to main lessons and then is back at home. We'll keep him on governors report to keep that '*threat*' up there so he knows it's the last boundary. Mr. Locks and I would also like you to come in on Mondays and Fridays for reviews so we can work hard together at getting him through and maybe every morning or after school for the first few weeks so we can keep on top of daily incidents."

I sat and let this wash over me for a second. How the hell was I supposed to do that and keep my job? "Have you done a new timetable yet?" I asked, "I mean…has all this been put into motion and ready to go?"

She bought it out of the folder and I glanced over it week by week. There was a whole day that he wasn't even *in* school and others where there were just one or two lessons starting around 10 am. If I wasn't there to make him get up and go to school then I knew he probably wouldn't bother. Brendon truly believed he could pass his exams with no effort and saw revision and course work as an unnecessary pain.

"Janice..I'm going to have to seriously consider this.

You have to give me a few days because it will affect my life massively."

"I understand," she replied, "but if there *are* ways round it then I really think it's for the best. The best way forward for Brendon. To be honest…" she paused, "I don't think the school are going to give you any other option. If you want him to make it through this last hurdle and get through his GCSE's then this is going to be the only way."

She printed me off a copy of the revised timetable that they wanted to implement after next week and a copy of his letter to Victor Churchman for posterity before going to fetch Brendon so we could all have a discussion together. He came in and gave me a big hug. "I love you Mommy." He sat down next to me and began drumming his fingers on the table.

"Brendon," Janice started, "We need to discuss a couple of things, the first one being an email you sent to the MP Victor Churchman?"

"Oh yeah. His secretary replied back to me the other day and said he'd look into it."

"Well, he actually came into school the other day to see Mr. Fothergill."

"And?" said Brendon, wondering what the big deal was.

"Well, do you not think it would have been better for you to address these problems with senior staff like Mr. Locks or Mr. Fothergill before you went directly to your local MP?"

"Err, No. Since when do they EVER listen to me?

Besides, I've probably done this school a favour now and they'll get better software."

To be honest, as I sat and listened, I really couldn't come up with any argument against his justification. Janice and I looked at each other in silent agreement.

"And Business Studies," she continued, "what you said to Mr. Jenkins about him being a teacher because he hasn't the ability to be in business?"

"Well it's true," he stated.

"Whatever you may believe Brendon, that was a hurtful and disrespectful comment that has no merit."

"Mr. Jenkins has never explained *anything* to do with business, EVER. He hasn't got a clue and all he does is refer you to a text book. That's not teaching. I can read a book at home."

Whilst I recognised his rudeness, part of me agreed with his argument. I was beginning to wonder if Aspergers was catching.

Janice went through the proposed new timetable with Brendon, explaining that I would be coming in if I could, on a daily basis. He didn't really seem to be bothered either way apart from the fact he got a whole day off and could use that to play on his computer. Aspie kids didn't revise at home. I'd been told this by the SEN team when I'd been struggling to get him to do homework. Home is for home and work is for work and never the twain shall meet.

Brendon said he had to go because he was hungry and needed to get to the canteen before his next lesson. He ruffled my hair on his way out and disappeared.

"I'll let you know what I can do in the next few days." I said to Janice as I stood up to leave.

She rubbed my shoulder. "I know it's hard. You know where I am and we'll talk soon."

I drove home wondering how the hell I could manage Brendon's new timetable, daily school meetings and stay at work. It wasn't possible. It would be easy to say no to the school but if I didn't accommodate them would they see that as neglect on my part? Would they have further excuses to get him out? Besides, I'd spent four and a half years fighting his corner, I couldn't just give up at the last hurdle. This was the time he really needed me so he could have something to show for the brilliant mind that he had and finish school with decent qualifications.

I got back and decided I should talk to Karl. He would help me decide what to do or give me some alternatives. Plus he needed to know the next stage we were at since the governors meeting. His phone rang a few times and I was expecting the Bond style answer machine to kick in when it was answered by someone else.

"Hello…" said a young female voice at the other end. It floored me a little.

"Err.. hello, is Karl available please?" I asked the girl. The girl I recognised as Sarah.

"No he's indisposed at the moment and he'll be busy for most of the day. Can I take a message?"

Indisposed. Really.

"Can you ask him to ring Sophie, please?" I replied politely, biting extremely hard on my lower lip.

"*Who*, sorry?" She schmoozed. I really wasn't in the mood for this little game.

"SO-PHIE." I replied loud and clear. "And when he's finished being indisposed please tell him I need to speak to him as a matter of urgency because I've just received a letter from the clinic and it looks like he's contracted a sexually transmitted disease."

CHAPTER 16

Within two hours of me arriving home and munching through the family sized bar of chocolate I'd bought at the garage on my way back, I got the phone call from Karl.

I knew he was going to be pissed off. Quite frankly I didn't give a toss.

"Rhodes, Sophie Rhodes." I answered, just to be extra childish.

"So, apparently I have an STD? That's a nice professional message to leave with one of my reps, Soph," he said flatly.

"Well, maybe your reps should be a touch more professional themselves when they answer your phone." I broke off another piece of Galaxy chocolate and shoved it into my mouth.

"I'm away at an exhibition and left my phone on the table whilst I was at the bar."

"And Sarah kindly answered it for you. She's *such* a sweetheart."

"I don't have time for this crap, I'm busy. I'll talk.."

"WAIT!" I said loudly, "before you go off and get

indisposed again, I have to go through something important. It's about Brendon."

"Make it quick. You have five minutes." Whilst I seriously had the urge to tell him to go to hell, I knew that wouldn't help. I hated how he spoke to me like a subordinate.

I explained the incident with the MP coming in and told him how they wanted to change Brendon's whole timetable and remove him from certain lessons where he was proving most difficult.

"The thing is, they want me to go in on a daily basis and I'd need to be at home on his part time days or I wouldn't trust him to go in. I don't know what to do…I need to help him but if I do, it means I can't do my job anymore."

I'd thought about this for the last couple of hours, trying to find ways I could make the two marry together. It was impossible. This was one of those hideous dilemmas that even a coin toss couldn't decide.

"Well you *can't* just jack your bloody job in. This is the problem with that school, they make inchoate plans without any thought on how it's going to affect anyone else." I heard him cover the mouthpiece of his phone and whisper to someone.

"*Hello?*" I called through my mobile.

"Sorry, like I said, I'm busy."

"I know it's not that simple Karl but I have to do what they say or everything I've done or you've done for him in the past has been for nothing. It's like I have no choice.

I may have to go part time but that will affect me massively, financially."

He wouldn't like that because the house I lived in was still half his and he'd always viewed it as a major investment. My earnings being reduced might mean it would have to be sold too early and put pay to the nice chunk of cash he would get if it was held on to for a few more years and gained more capital.

"This is ridiculous. You can't make snap shot decisions like that. The house needs to be paid for or neither of us will benefit." I heard the mellifluous tones of Sarah saying something to him in the background.

"I need to go..we will have to talk about this later." He hung up and I was left no nearer to a decision than before I'd spoken to him and to be honest it was looking like one I'd have to make alone.

I got the red leather notebook that I'd sullied last week with my phone box ideas and decided to make a for and against list. This could now become my stupid ideas and dilemma book. The process of writing things down usually made the route obvious; unless it was about shoes. In that case buy them all.

I drew a line down the centre of the next new page. Reasons to help Brendon and reasons to not. I took a deep breath and began to fill in the columns.

After I'd completed the pro's and con's I decided to take a break and come back to it later with fresh eyes. I felt weary and confused with nobody around to help me and my problems seemed insurmountable. I went to my word game for reprieve. An escape to the ether where my ubiquitous issues couldn't penetrate. I hurried to 'The Voice' as I hadn't been to play since he'd said "It's perfect" to my picture.

SOPHISTICATION: *Well that's good. I aim to please.*

I didn't really know what else to say. I scrolled back through our previous chat messages and felt a warmth and peculiar fizz. I hadn't felt that feeling in a long time and it unnerved me a little.

He was online.

THE VOICE: *You pleased me.*

Oh God. I did? There was that feeling again.

SOPHISTICATION: *Well I'm glad of that.*

Well at least I was pleasing someone, which made a bloody change.

THE VOICE: *Well I'm glad you're glad.*

SOPHISTICATION: *Ok, enough.:)*

The back and forth awkward conversation was becoming more puerile than that of a pair of year seven pupils.

I tried to concentrate on the actual play a bit more as I recognised I was just placing anything on the board to get to the chat quicker rather than be competitive. That was usually so unlike me.

THE VOICE: Texting in these little bubbles can be annoying sometimes don't you agree?

What did he mean by that? He didn't want to talk anymore? I felt a sudden surge of fear.

SOPHISTICATION: What, you don't want to talk anymore you mean?

I pressed send before I had chance to review the message. It sounded a tad desperate.

THE VOICE: Yes. That's exactly what I want to do. I want to talk.

I really didn't understand what he was on about. Was I missing something?

SOPHISTICATION: Well, isn't that what we are doing?

THE VOICE: No. I want to actually talk to you. I prefer real time conversations.

I suddenly went into free fall panic. Did he mean like *real* talking? As in 'on the phone' or something? I couldn't cope with that right now and I didn't know what to say. I was scared; terrified of not living up to the player behind the virtual board. At least on there I had a modicum of control. What if I was flummoxed or too nervous to talk? I mean this wasn't just anyone, this was 'The Voice'. It was HIM.

I placed my phone gently on the table and tried to calm down. I felt flustered and heady with a stomach full of manic butterflies. What the hell was wrong with me?

I decided to leave The Voice well alone for now until I'd had chance to work through my feelings. Generally when I acted in the heat of the moment it didn't go too well. I went back to my study and reviewed the list I'd been working on earlier.

All of a sudden, it was painfully clear. I had to be there for my son. I was his Mother and that was my main responsibility. If *I* didn't stick my neck out, then nobody else would and if I didn't sacrifice my time for him and he failed, could I live with that?

No. I couldn't. There was only one answer. I was going to have to leave my job.

CHAPTER 17

Giving up my job was neither an easy decision or a practical one. Never mind the fact I was about to go on a vacation to territories unknown. The expense of just maintaining a roof over our heads with heat and light was enough despite anything else. I still had to earn enough money but now it had to be from a flexible basis. The only way I could do that was to go freelance. I figured I knew enough people in this city to be able to make it work and whilst I wouldn't get the cherry pickings or the high flyers salary, I should at the very least be able to pay my way. It would be tight but I could do it.

Having gone through all my expenses I realised my car would be one of the first things that had to go, it was too dear to maintain and I could manage with a cheap jalopy to get me around. As I wandered through the house going about my business, I began to see everything with fresh eyes. I had *so* many unnecessary things. Loads of stuff I didn't need: nice clothes and shoes, ornaments and pictures and so on that I could sell at car boots or on eBay as extra bonus money. I'm sure I'd heard that some people had become eBay millionaires. You never knew. I'd worked out all the finances on a spread sheet: what I'd need to earn as a minimum and what I'd have to sacrifice so it worked. I'd done this not just for myself but for Karl so I could justify my decision when I eventually told him. He'd expect that at the very least. Having lived with Brendon I was learning the tactics of being ten steps ahead.

In order to put my plan into action I decided to put my car in the Auto-trader. Where intention goes, energy flows! It would be a good start and an insight to my selling ability. Damn, I thought, I'd better get it washed as it looked like a shed. I got my keys and made to go to the chaps that ran the hand car wash down the road. Then I stopped and thought about that. No! If was going to do this properly then every penny counted and I shouldn't waste or squander on anything.

"It can't be that hard to wash a mini." I said out loud to myself. Turns out I was wrong. I couldn't understand how I'd managed to make more smears than before I'd started and spent for *ever* trying to rub them away with a chamois leather. And alloys – they were hellish! Fair play to the blokes at the wash and wax that did this for a living for it was no mean feat and they fully deserved the measly fiver they charged. The only good thing about the ordeal was that I found a lost bottle of Kenzo Flower perfume, seven hair bobbles, an invite to a party and £3.75 under my seats when I was hoovering the inside. Still, it looked way better than it had in weeks. I went and got my camera and took several shots so I could place my online advert. I put it in the Auto-trader for a month and then rang my friend in advertising at the local city newspaper and got it in there for the weekend. Done.

Now I needed to talk to my boss.

I drove my smeary, yet clean mini into the city and all the while kept going through a mock conversation with Colin out loud in my car. I arrived at the office and saw Johnno at his desk who gave me a big smile when he clocked me coming through the doors.

"Soph! I thought you weren't in until tomorrow!" He stood up and limped over.

"Really? It's still hurting?" I started laughing. But inside I felt wretched. I was hardly ever going to see him or anybody I worked with when I left. These people were like my other family.

"Why are you here? Get bored? Oh wait! I got you a present…" He hobbled back to his desk and opened his drawer. He put the crinkly package behind his back and came over to me.

I stood there waiting and smiling. He was so cute.

"There!" He handed me a box of Waitrose chocolate brownies.

"Ha Ha! Funny!"

"What? I heard you liked them? "He stood staring at me with a schoolboy grin on his face.

"Well, I'm so glad I've been the subject of your amusement." I took the cakes and slung them onto my desk. "Now I have to see Colin, I'll be back in a bit." I walked to my Editors office and felt the fear and sadness rising within and began to question whether I was doing the right thing or not.

He was on the phone to Trudie, I could tell. I went to walk away but he looked surprised to see me and nodded for me to take a seat. I sat there running my planned speech through my mind and digging my nails into each of my finger beds in turn.

"I can't Trudie, no. Babe it's just not a good time. I'm sorry, no. I have to go." I watched him end the call and sigh. He shook his head. "You'd think I'd get better at choosing women wouldn't you? Anyway, back early Soph?" He smiled but looked a bit sad.

"Are you OK?" I asked.

"Ugh..Relationships..difficult women. The usual nightmare." He threw his phone on the desk.

I knew right then and there that Trudie was not going to be a keeper.

"So, good to have you back. Get everything sorted?"

Oh God. I felt sick and like I was going to cry. I felt the heat rising from nowhere and found it impossible to maintain contact with Colin's soulful blue eyes.

"Yes and no, "I said slowly, "Colin.. I can't do my job anymore.." That was not how I had planned to say it but that's how it came out.

"What do you mean? " He sat very still and just stared at me.

"I mean, I'm going to have to leave. I don't want to but I have to. It's the school...it's not me...well it's my decision too but...

"Soph…calm down. Start again. He pushed an empty glass towards me and filled it full of soda water and remained forward in his chair, looking puzzled.

"Brendon's timetable has been slashed due to his behaviour and I have to go in and monitor his days. They only want him to attend minimum lessons to get through his exams and then go home. They want my help on a daily basis and If I don't comply, they'll kick him out, I'm sure." I blew the air out of my mouth, allowing the angst to free itself and then I felt my eyes welling up.

The room stayed silent and warm. Very warm.

"It's not what I *want* to do but it's what *I have* to do". I looked down at my lap because I wanted to hold back the tears and could feel them making a bid for freedom.

"It seems a bit drastic, Soph," Colin said softly. "I really don't want you to go."

I looked up at his face, all forlorn and dazed. "I know. I don't want to. I love my job but look at me Colin…I'm already having too much time off because of this and it's now going to get worse. I thought if I could get some freelance work from different publications, companies and from *here* of course…"

"Soph, I would throw all sorts your way, if that's what you choose to do, but you know it's usually just reviews on restaurants, clubs and shows that we farm out. Is that *really* what you want to be doing? Plus I'd have to fill your position with somebody else, you know that?"

"Yes. I know that." I placed the envelope I'd been clutching in my hand that contained my letter of resignation in front of him before I tore it into pieces. "Here's my notice." I said weakly.

He didn't even pick it up. Another long silence stretched between us. "Sophie, I'm not going to even look at this until I leave tomorrow night. I want you to go home and think it over a bit longer. Take tomorrow off. If I don't hear from you by the end of play then I'll accept your resignation even though it's not what I want."

"OK." I stood up quickly. "Thanks Colin." He watched silently as I hurried out of his office and the tears fell from my eyes. I saw Johnno stare after me as I left crying. I couldn't even begin to deal with that now. I was going to miss this place and these people way more than I could have possibly realised and the enormity of that threatened to knock me to the floor if I didn't keep walking.

Chapter 18

I got back home to find Brendon in the kitchen cutting into a t-shirt. Not any t-shirt but a brand new, Lacoste polo shirt.

"What the hell are you doing?" I dropped my bag and went to snatch it from him.

"Fuck off!" he shouted, pulling it away, "I'm taking the label out the back because it does my head in. It irritates the back of my neck." He was hacking too close to the fabric and about to ruin a very expensive top. This explained all the tears in the back of his other shirts that I'd noticed when I was ironing them. I'd forgotten to ask him why they all had gaping holes across the back seams, but now I knew.

"Let me do it, you're going to cut it into shreds. It's expensive." I urged.

He threw it down on the kitchen counter along with the scissors. I rescued it quickly and began gently teasing at the stitches.

"What's wrong with you? You look like you've been crying," he said brusquely.

"Well, I have. I've just handed my notice in to work and I'm very upset."

"What for? Are you retarded? How are we going to have any money? That's a bit selfish."

I wanted to slap him. How dare he. I put down the Lacoste shirt I'd been carefully trying to remove the label from. The prized label that *most* people bought the damn named shirt for in the first place.

"*I'm* selfish. Are you *serious?* Well, Brendon, maybe if you had tried just to keep your mouth shut and your opinions to yourself I wouldn't have to. I'm doing this to make sure you stay in school for the next six months and pass your exams. I'm doing this because YOUR timetable has been slashed, because YOU have been removed from lessons and YOU need to start getting your head round this because I'll be coming in every day to make sure that YOUR behaviour is kept inline."

"Whatever. You're just lazy." He pushed past me, put on his coat and left the house slamming the front door so hard I sensed the vibrations under my feet.

I felt the onset of angry tears and the heat rising from my chest and filling my cheeks. I went into the hall and kicked off my shoes. I noticed the pretty stained glass in the front door had cracked some more. A few more slams and that would come crashing to the floor like everything else.

I went back into the kitchen and opened the fridge looking for something to eat. Stress eating relief. Instead I saw a chilled bottle of vintage rose. I pulled it out and placed it on the counter and watched as its curved glass neck began to cover in a sweat of condensation. I uncorked the bottle and breathed in the scent of sunbathed, under ripe berries and freshly picked wild flowers. If a lovers' picnic could have a scent, that would be it, I thought, as I poured the pale blush into a large glass. I never tired of hearing the first few glugs of liquid as it freed itself from the narrow neck of the bottle. I almost wanted to pour it back in and do it again. I took several, undignified slugs and let out a deep breath.

What a shit day.

I wasn't going to change my mind about leaving work despite Colin making me feel like staying. I'd never get a boss like that again. Now I'd told Brendon I may as well tell Karl too and get it all over with. I looked at my watch. It was 6.20pm. Bryony would be back at 7-ish so I should ring him now whilst I had the house to myself. I took my wine glass and bottle with me to the study and fired up my computer. I'd need the spreadsheets I'd done, up on view, so I could answer anything he threw at me. If he answered of course. Maybe it would be the dancing doll and I'd get to tell her instead.

"Hi Soph." He answered. I could hear the car roaring and streams of traffic behind him.

"Hi. The reason for the call is just to let you know that I handed my notice in today and I thought you should know." There. I'd done it.

"Tell me you're fucking joking..*please*.." His voice was heightened and raspy.

I took another swallow of pink juice.

"No, I'm not joking. I've made the decision to support Brendon and I can't do both. But before you start going mental I've made a plan and a spreadsheet. I should be able to get enough freelance work to be just about OK. Plus I've put my car up for sale and I've changed the utility providers for the house so that's cheaper and I've looked into changing the house insurance when it's due next month. I've got loads I can sell, you know, like an eBay hobby. I've thought it through." I said finishing and taking another slow sip of my chilled wine.

"You've thought it through? *Thought it through?* It's the most monumentally, stupid decision I've ever known you make. Without any concerns for the financial impact that's going to have on everyone else. I can't afford to bail you out! I have more than enough expenses!"

"I haven't asked you to bail me out," I snapped, but he wasn't listening.

"And how the fuck are we going to cover the mortgage and the council tax, the bills, the food and every other bloody thing. That property is a pension fund to me, to US and you've just killed it."

"Like I said, I've made a spreadsheet. I can just about meet my fair share."

"A spreadsheet. Right. Well that I'd LOVE to see that! A spreadsheet showing the future going up in smoke. Fucking unbelievable. You've left us high and dry. I *suggest* you rescind your notice rather sharpish."

To say that I fucking hated him right then would have been a colossal understatement.

"No Karl, I will not rescind my notice because I am putting my child first. That's what parents do. And, with respect, I haven't left us high and dry, that's what you did when you walked out on this family. When you decided it was just *too* much pressure. This is what I'm doing. End of. I'm sorry that doesn't fit with your little agenda but bad luck. I'm the one here, dealing with the everyday shit, taking the abuse, making everything work so I think I'm MORE than entitled to make my own decisions on what's right for my family." My breathing was rapid with heightened emotion but I had a deadly, bone chilling control that seemed to be taking hold of me.

"Don't turn this round on me!" he scoffed, "you're the one making 'silly girl' decisions and changing everything and causing a workable situation to become difficult. What you're doing is idiotic. And for the record I didn't *walk out* on my family, as you put it, I left an environment that was impossible to function in."

"Impossible to function in? I seem to have to do it Karl. I HAVE to because you didn't. And you can dress it up however you like. You. Walked. Out."

"Because I couldn't live like that anymore. Not because I didn't love my family. Not because I didn't love you. That was the hardest thing for me!"

"Well, you didn't love us enough." I ended the call with a defiant press on the red button because it was going nowhere and I was sick of how he was talking to me. I couldn't be bothered with the drama, the excuses or the blame. But I knew one thing. I was going to make this work even if I had to starve myself to death.

He didn't call back which was a good thing because I

wouldn't have answered. It was rare I cut a call to anyone but if I did, ringing me back and expecting me to answer was futile. Karl knew that. I had no doubt he'd come back for more soon enough.

Brendon and Bryony both came through the door laughing, having picked each other up on the street outside. As soon as Bryony saw me she came and gave me a big hug. She smelt of cheap teen perfume and jelly sweets.

"Oh Mum, are you OK?" She hugged me tight. "I heard you packed your job in."

"Yep. It's not going down too well with people," I replied into her hair.

"Because it's stupid, " said Brendon. "*My names Mom…* DUHHHHH." He was laughing as he said it, but I didn't find it funny.

"She's doing it for *you,* Brendon!"

"You dizzy blud?" Brendon lifted Bryony from my hug and tipped her upside down. She wailed and beat her arms on his leg to be put down.

"Well at least you're in a better mood," I remarked sarcastically, "does anyone want any dinner?"

"Nope had mine at Jessie's," Brendon replied. Well that explained the lift.

"And I've been to MacDonald's with everyone," said Bryony. I didn't class that as food but she was content enough and I was more than happy with my liquid equivalent after today.

I went into the living room and sat in the corner of my sofa and curled my legs up. I shut my eyes and just tried to *be* for a minute or two. Thoughts were whizzing round my mind and I couldn't make them stop. I'd never been very good at that *'Just empty your mind'* thing.

I clicked open my word game. 'The Voice' had wanted real time conversation. Maybe it would be nice to talk. I really liked him and he was so far removed from all the other stress in my life. Like a warm hand in the darkness.

SOPHISTICATION: Do you mean on the phone?

I typed in quickly before I changed my mind.

It was lunchtime there. It was a good fifteen minutes before he responded.

THE VOICE: Yes. That's the usual practice.

Well of course it was. *Why* did I say that?

SOPHISTICATION: Yes, quite.

THE VOICE: So would you like to? Talk on the phone?

I felt all nervous again. But yes. Of course I did.

SOPHISTICATION: Yes. Why not.

THE VOICE: You don't have to sound so enthusiastic.

As I was reading his last message and thinking I should have sounded a little more eager, Brendon came in the living room with a film.

"Think we should watch Fight Club," he said as he went to put it in the DVD player.

"I've seen it before."

"Yes Mommy, but it's my favourite film and I thought I'd come and cheer you up."

I loved how he thought cheering me up involved doing something that *he* wanted to do.

"Well, if you like…" I guessed a bit of Brad Pitt wouldn't hurt and it was a cracking movie. Plus it was rather relevant since I'd been in my own little fight club all day. As the film came to play I went back to my game for a second.

SOPHISTICATION: I am. Really. Let's arrange something.

THE VOICE: Well there's no time like the present.

What? Did he mean right now?

"Mum! Put your game down. The film's starting. This is about spending quality time with your son."

SOPHISTICATION: I can't now. I'm watching a film.

"MUM! Put it down or I'll take it off you."

I put it down. I'd go back to him when the film finished. Maybe we could talk then. I spent the next two and a half hours curled next to my boy who was trying to make amends for his earlier outburst in his own sweet way.

Brendon went to bed as the credits came up on the TV and I went to the kitchen to make a drink. I took my phone and clicked on my game.

THE VOICE: Wow. You're. Watching. A. Film.

Whoa. What was that supposed to mean? Slightly unfriendly. I hadn't called him an arsehole for a long time but he was heading back in that direction. That actually hurt my feelings.

SOPHISTICATION: Yes I was. But it's finished now.

Let's see if he suggests a call now.

THE VOICE: Well I hope you enjoyed it.

Jesus. What's this all about?

SOPHISTICATION: Yes I did thank you. Did I do something to upset you?

THE VOICE: Well most people would pause a movie to talk to their friends. I'm sure you must have a remote that facilitates that.

Really? Why was he being so cutting?

SOPHISTICATION: Well I was watching it with my son.

THE VOICE: Well I hope he enjoyed it.

SOPHISTICATION: Yes. He did thank you.

Clearly I'd totally racked him off without even trying, just because I wasn't able to talk precisely when he wanted to. But I couldn't. Welcome to Aspergers. He didn't know that, but maybe he should be a little more mindful that others lives weren't necessarily as easy.

THE VOICE: Good.

That was it? Good? I was so upset and annoyed. In fact, I felt cyber violated. Why was everyone being so mean to me today?

I threw my phone across the settee and thought about Karl and The Voice and the demands that Fothergill had put into place. I couldn't please anyone, no matter what I tried to do for the best. Everyone had their own bloody agendas. I pulled at the newly formed ladder in my tights and watched as it crept up my leg and the fine, denier strands became taught against my exposed flesh.

CHAPTER 19

Within ten days of selling on the online marketplace I'd had my eBay account barred. Clearly I wasn't cut out to become an eBay millionaire. Being naive to this arena I had put some of my clothes on there without a reserve price because I didn't know what that was. I was already finding the efforts of listing stuff a massive time sink and wondering how the hell anyone made money from it. I'd sold a Calvin Klein skirt, a Karen Millen dress and a Coach jacket for £3.00.

Your eBay items have sold! Speciallady72 has paid and items need to be shipped.

Err, no they don't, I thought. Are you kidding me? £3.00. That lot alone had set me back in excess of £600.00 and she wanted it all for £3.00? Pfft! I'd rather give it to charity or my daughter than sell it for that! I found that I could send a message to the buyer and decided to tell her that the deal was off. Surely she'd expect that anyway.

EBay message to Speciallady72 -from Sophistication04:
Sorry but I've changed my mind about the sale and I've sent you a paypal refund. Cheers.:)

Speciallady72- You are bound by the trading standard to honour the sale. Please notify so I can pay again as I won those items.

Sophistication04 – No can do – they're too expensive to go for £3.00 and I wouldn't be able to live with myself. Sorry.

Speciallady72 – Then I will have to report you for unfair trading. That's bad practice.

Sophistication04 – Knock yourself out. Sorry.

Report me to whom? What were they going to do, arrest me? Instead they barred my account. Awesome.

Apart from screwing up eBay I'd managed to make a brilliant shopping budget and save loads of money on other things. I'd seen a TV talk show one morning with an MP on there saying that people could save an awful lot of money by visiting all the supermarkets and bagging their BOGOF offers. I was sure he didn't have to do that but I decided to give it a go. I'd visited Morrisons, Asda, Sainsburys and Tesco and kept myself strictly to the end of aisle offers. I had more cous cous than Ainsley Harriott and enough beans and Colgate sensitive toothpaste to get us up to Christmas.

I'd had three people look at my car and was sure one of those was going to buy it as they kept coming back to look it over with an endless supply of relatives, which was always a good sign. Colin had accepted my resignation with a heavy heart and I'd been spending the last two weeks at work being told that I could change my mind at anytime. I'd been close on several occasions. Johnno in particular, had made me want to kill myself. He kept leaving sticky notes on my desk with little messages or an occasional chocolate or love heart sweets saying 'Miss you' or 'Don't leave me' it was hilarious but heart wrenching. His latest move did have me reconsidering big time.

"If you stay at work I promise to get you a date with Frank Lampard," he said seriously.

"LOL! Really Johnno? What about his girlfriend, she may not be too pleased."

"I'll find a way, I mean it." I had to chuckle at his candour.

Colin had been brilliant and had rang around various publications and such getting me an 'in' on the freelance list and bigging me up to everyone he knew. I'd already started to get assignments and also some PR work for a company and that was before I'd legitimately left my current role. I knew I was going to make it and I hoped it was going to be worth the sacrifice.

I sat at my desk and looked around surveying the whole office. I wanted to take it all in so I could remember the atmosphere when I was no longer here: Monica was studying something intently on her computer screen and sucking a pen. She always had a pen in her mouth. The entertainment girls sat in a huddle discussing nightlife dressed for a party at any given minute. Johnno was on the phone, his desk covered in sports regalia and his Adidas bag, full of kit, at his side. I hoped Bryony ended up with someone like him. He was such a lovely lad.

I picked up one of the jelly beans that Johnno had left as today's present and clicked on my word game for the millionth time. The Voice hadn't responded to me since I'd not taken him up on the phone call. He'd played two goes, storming words, but had left no message. He hadn't, however taken a turn in the last four days. I was on the verge of heartbreak. I couldn't explain it but that's how it felt. Like I'd been dumped. I couldn't play until he did and I felt like he was holding me ransom. I just wanted him to talk to me. I'd left a message a couple of days ago in the chat bubble.

SOPHISTICATION: It's your go…

Nothing. No play. No response. I decided to send another. Maybe he wasn't well or something. I should be nicer.

SOPHISTICATION: Hey, are you alright? I hope so.

There, that was nice. I clicked it off and felt a sense of woe.

It was getting on for 4pm and I was leaving early as Colin and I were going to the World Service restaurant tonight. I felt privileged to be taken as his guest as it was a beautiful place set in a 17th century building and it would be a nice way to end our working relationship. Well, from a full time point of view. I went to his office to see him about the arrangements. He was standing up, analysing something on his computer, deep in thought.

"Colin..?" I snapped him out of his reverie.

"Yes babe. What's up?"

"What time shall I meet you tonight?"

"Starts at 6.30pm so how about 6pm at the Slug and Lettuce?"

"Yeah, that's great. I'll see you later." I slipped out and left him to his work.

When I arrived home and entered the hallway, I heard Brendon on his mobile to someone.

"You're a dickhead and if you don't sort it out I will never talk to you again. You're a fucking waste man." He ended the call and looked as angry as hell.

"Who are you talking to?"

"Luke. Shithead," he snapped.

"You really don't have to swear all the time you know. You are quite capable of stringing a sentence together without profanity. You're not a complete reprobate."

"I'm an articulate reprobate, Mother."

"What's he done to upset you?" I asked carefully. Usually he'd tell me everything. Often things I didn't want to know and information that teenage boys should keep to themselves. I never knew if he did it for the shock factor or because it was how he was.

"He's put two things up for sale on eBay that he didn't even have. Anyway, a couple of kids have bought them and he's taken the money but obviously not sent the goods because they don't exist. You can't fucking do that to people."

"That's *terrible*. I hope he's going to give them the money back," I said somewhat concerned.

"Well I'm not talking to him unless he does and I want proof that he's done it. If he doesn't I'm going to smack him one."

Brendon had a very keen sense of right and wrong which was amazing since he couldn't apply it to himself. He was often in trouble around school for interfering in fights or stopping teachers from shouting at pupils. He was like a real life vigilante: Judge, jury and executioner. He would have made the perfect Judge Dredd.

"You can't hit people and I know you won't," I said, "but he should not be being fraudulent to people." I considered my own misdemeanour on eBay but at least I'd refunded the special lady.

"Yeah, but he doesn't need to know that and I feel like punching him."

His phone beeped and he looked down at another message. "Ugh.." He said out loud to it. "Are all girls this needy? I'm sick of getting constant texts, it's pissing me off."

"Yes, Brendon they are, especially if they like you. Get used to it and be nice. She's a lovely girl and you're very lucky."

I went upstairs and jumped in the shower ready to go on my evening junket. I chose a simple black dress from Whistles that was always a winner and one of the few things that hadn't made it to my eBay pile. I called a taxi and waited for it with a nice glass of wine as I changed over handbags. I walked round in bare stockinged feet until the taxi arrived as my black court shoes were going to kill me, I knew it. Thank God I'd be mostly sitting down.

I shouted goodbye to the kids and added a "And do not ring me unless it's absolutely necessary Brendon! I'm out with my boss and I'll be back when I'm back!"

The Slug and Lettuce was relatively busy but I spotted Colin in an instant. He had that edgy style that just set him apart from everyday people. He was wearing a dark, navy Paul Smith suit and Pale blue shirt. He looked effortlessly classic.

"You look great!" I grinned, "that really brings your eye colour out."

"Thanks Soph, and back at ya! I got you a vodka and coke..You still drink that right?"

"I'll drink anything Colin. And yes I do. Thanks!" I'd not had a vodka and coke for ages and I made a mental note to rectify that.

We talked about work for a while and then had to hurry to the restaurant.

There were a few people I recognised on the guest list when we arrived- Paul Hymes being one of them. He came straight over to Colin and shook his hand and planted a kiss on mine when I went to shake it. I wiped it off on the side of my dress as soon as he let go and focussed his attention on my boss.

We got seated at a nice table near the window and got ready for our food. It was a pre-set three course meal to sample their new menu.

Almond flaked prawns, chilled garlic and almond puree, compressed grapes.

Derbyshire filet of beef, World Service béarnaise, crispy onion, goose fat chips.

Yoghurt foam, pumpkin seeds, sour cherry sorbet and /or an assiette of desserts for two.

A bottle of house red and white wine were already on the table. I hit the red instantly. I was going to make the most of this meal as this kind of thing was now decadence to me and would serve to be a memory of the good old days.

The food was outstanding as was the service and I loved it in this place. Colin and I got through the wine with ease and ordered another bottle. We spent the evening chatting and laughing about all sorts of things from the boring to the ridiculous. We even explored my phone box idea a little further and how we could set it up. It got more absurd the more we drank but we talked about it like it was a new and exciting venture.

"Shall we have some champagne?" Colin asked, as he poured the last of the wine into our glasses. I was already feeling warm and tingly which didn't help with my ability to say no.

"Oh, go on then," I said with a big grin, "So how's Trudie?"

"Soph! I was having a really good night 'till then!"

I started giggling. "Sorry."

"Meh. She's been encouraged to move on."

"Colin! We need to find you the right woman. They're always amazing anyway so what is it that's missing?"

"He leant forward, elbow on the table and a finger on his lips as he pretended to ponder this question. "Hmmm…" he looked at me across the table. "The X factor."

I laughed. "Ok Simon Cowell, and what *IS* your X factor?"

He looked at me very seriously for a few seconds. I wondered if I'd upset him a little by asking too many personal questions. I really shouldn't drink so much.

"It's an unquantifiable thing Soph. Let's go and research it. Come on! Let's go to the office with this champers and watch a film and make plans for phone boxes and figure out the X factor! I need to get out of here now." He picked up the bottle and made his way to say thank you to the owner.

I sat there surprised. Well OK then. Colin was obviously as tipsy as me!

We made our way down the street, arms linked and laughing at our own stupidity. We got to the office and through the glass doors.

"What's the alarm, Soph?"

"What? Err… 2, 0, 4, 9…" it took me a while to remember. "You should know that Colin!"

"I do. I just want to make sure you're awake." He giggled as he punched in the numbers and we went through the office doors. It seemed weird to see it all dark and quiet. I followed Colin through to his office and he put the wall lights on.

"Music!" he said out loud to himself as he opened iTunes on his computer. "Go get glasses Soph, we have the world to save!"

I went to the kitchen and looked for glasses. I couldn't find them so I got two mugs instead.

"Mugs?! You philistine, Sophie Rhodes!" Colin went to pour the champagne into them anyway as we stood at his desk. We lifted our mugs and knocked them together as The Kings of Leon played in the background.

"Here's to..stuff.." I said.

"Stuff?! I can't believe I let you write for me," he smirked, "here's to the mysteries of life, Sophie."

I raised the mug to my mouth and took a great big mouthful of champagne. The bubbles exploded tenfold in my mouth and burst forth, spilling down my chin and onto my dress.

"Arrr…" I squealed, bending forward and trying to brush the fizzing liquid off my Whistles frock. My hair had fallen into my face and strands had stuck to my champagne lips. I felt Colin's hand gently remove my hair and tuck it behind my ear. I looked up at him as he very slowly took the mug from my hand and put it on the desk, not once taking his eyes from mine. His hand came to my face as he stepped closer and rubbed his thumb softly over my wet lips before he lowered his mouth onto mine.

Chapter 20

Colin's hands cupped my face as he gently kissed me, slowly exploring my mouth. My head was spinning with a million fuzzy thoughts but I didn't pull away from him. He broke away smoothly, his face still close to mine, his lips millimetres away as he looked down into my eyes. I was dizzy and breathless and didn't know if it was the result of the wine or I was actually swooning. Maybe this was a bad idea. He was my boss. OK, soon to be ex boss but I'd still be working on and off for him. My head was saying stop but my body was screaming go for gold.

"Colin…I don't think…"

"No. Don't think," he whispered, as he lowered his mouth to mine again. This time his kiss was harder. His hand travelled to the nape of my neck, twisting my hair between his fingers. He pulled firmly on my tousled locks forcing my head back and pressing his mouth down with more passion; his tongue teased and sought out mine, probing and playful. I played back. I was lost in his kiss, becoming submissive to his need. His hand slowly slid down my stretched neck and over the veil like fabric of my dress and softly glanced over my breast. It was momentary, but I felt my body respond to his touch. My back arched slightly, pushing me into his solid abdomen, the yearning in the depths of my core building in waves of rampant desire. He released my hair and moved both hands gradually down my sides, following the contours of my body, over my hips where he held me firmly and pulled me closer to him. I felt him hard against me and my body pulsated with want. He gathered the fine material of my dress up to my hips. I felt the fabric tickle my outer thighs as it moved up over the fine denier of my 'hold up' stockings. Artful hands moved to the rear of my body and squeezed the round flesh of my buttocks. He buried his head into the curve of my neck as it met my shoulder, sucking and biting gently on my warm skin and lifted me up effortlessly, seating me on the edge of his desk, sweeping papers to the floor with no regard. He parted my knees and moved his body in-between me as he ran his palms up my stockinged legs, pausing where the sheer nylon met the soft naked flesh of my inner thighs. I felt my limbs begin to tremble as they gripped his hips and I slid my fingers just under the waistband of his trousers, moving them to meet together at the buckle of his belt which I started to undo with deliberate slowness.

"Oh, Soph…" he groaned. He reached round to the back of my dress and undid the zip inch by inch as we both stared wantonly at each other. His soulful blue eyes now looked more needy and the same navy blue colour of his suit. I took a sharp intake of breath as he pulled the dress from my shoulders and let the material fall in folds at my elbows. I could feel my heart beating in every part of my body.

"Oh my God…" I whispered as I gazed upon his parted lips. He stared down at me and I could feel his breath, hot on my face as he drank me in.

Chapter 21

I woke up with a start just before my alarm went off and for a split second I felt normal. Then it all came back to me in a nasty flash and I felt like a slovenly whore. Jesus Christ, I slept with my boss. I sat up in bed and tried to collect my thoughts which proved extremely difficult in my hungover state.

"Oh.My.God." I kept repeating out loud as remnants of the evening came flooding back to me. How the hell was I going to deal with going to work today? What a hideous nightmare. I remembered it being well past 2.30 am when I'd finally got home. Colin had insisted on riding back with me in the cab to make sure I got there safely, which was nice of him. As I'd made to get out the car he'd pulled me back and kissed me long and slow, not giving a toss about the waiting taxi driver. I remembered hoping that Brendon wasn't still up as he would have gone spare if he'd seen me with another bloke. As far as he was concerned my role was 'Mother to Brendon – end of story.' I was surprised he hadn't rang me, that was *most* unusual, but he'd left every single light in the house on like normal. I'd tiptoed around the various rooms switching off lights and closing doors, trying not to fall over and then deliberately falling into my welcoming bed with a stupid smile on my face. Next thing I knew I was here, in the bright light of morn, where everything didn't look quite so pretty.

I teetered downstairs and made some honey on toast. I wasn't that hungry but I needed sugary carbohydrates to make me feel better. And tea. Lots of it. I heard the thumping sounds of Brendon coming downstairs. He walked in and glared at me. He looked as shattered as I felt.

"Where the hell were you last night? What time did you get in?"

"Morning!" I smiled with fake cheeriness. I really didn't need the Spanish inquisition right now. "I can't remember," I lied, "it was fairly late."

"Well it was way after midnight when I went to bed… Why were you out with your boss so late?"

"It was an important restaurant review." The World Service menu paled into insignificance next to the desserts that had followed at the office. I experienced a sudden sense of thrill and fear as I thought about it.

After dropping the kids at school and making my way to work I spent the whole journey planning on how I was going to react to Colin. What I was going to say, how I was going to say it and how cool and composed I was going to be. I was thankful that this was my second to last day at work and this hadn't happened in the midst of my career. As I approached the office from the street I was reminded of last night, like I was doing the walk of shame. I was dreading going in. I felt like a naughty schoolgirl which was ridiculous and I urged myself to get a grip.

I walked into the office and said a general 'Good morning' to everyone around. I looked down the bottom of the corridor to Colin's office as I made my way to my desk. I saw him standing talking to someone on his mobile and he watched me as I made my way through. I broke my gaze away as I couldn't handle it. He was far enough away that I couldn't tell what he was thinking, thank God. I felt like a stupid, bloody teenager.

"Soph... You're nearly leaving..." said Johnno in a sad voice.

I smiled. "I've just bloody got here! Don't start upsetting me. But if you make me a coffee I'll visit you every week."

"Really?"

"I promise to do my best. I will *actually* miss you." I pulled a sad face and he wiped away a fake tear.

"OK I'll make you a coffee, but hold on, I've got you something." He went to his desk and brought back a Clinton's Card's bag.

I thanked him and opened it up to find a little grey teddy bear saying, Forever Friends.

"Awwww, Johnno that's so cute! I *love* him. You're the best friend anyone could ever have," I said sincerely. He was so nice. I watched him walk down the corridor, thankful I didn't have to make my own drink as the kitchen was past Colin's office and I couldn't face that yet. As Johnno walked by it I flicked my eyes over to see Colin still standing talking and still looking down towards my desk.

Jesus Christ, I thought.

I fired up my computer and went on my word game whilst I waited for it to spark into life.

The Voice still hadn't played. Nor left a message. I still felt sad and hurt when my expectation was flattened.

Johnno came back with my coffee.

"You're an angel," I said, as I brought the hot drink to my mouth.

"So how was the World Service? Colin said it was a great night."

"Yes it was very nice," I replied, thinking that 'Colin had said it was a *great* night,' and running that through my mind.

My desk phone buzzed and broke me out of my dream.

"Soph, can you come through for a minute?" Colin said through my earpiece.

My heart went into a mad aerobic rave and I was not sure my legs would carry me down the passageway. My brain kicked in as I made my way to his office. OK, this is it. Act as normal as possible. You're a grown up. A woman of the world. It's just one of those things. Normal. Everyday occurrence. Loads of people do this kind of thing.

He was sat at his desk, nice and calm, with a happy smile. I glanced very quickly into his eyes, unable to keep up the eye contact. As I sat down, I saw the champagne bottle in the corner of the room and felt my cheeks flush a little. Oh God.

I shuffled in his leather chair playing with my hands in my lap and wanting to burst out laughing with anxiety.

"So, how do you feel?" He tilted his head on one side and smiled.

"A bit rough to be honest." This was excruciating already. How was he so together?

"Soph…" He waited until I looked up. "How do you feel…about last night?"

Here we go. The about last night speech.

"Great film. One of Rob Lowe's finest I think," I replied, using humour, as usual, to get me out of a difficult conversation.

"Soph…How do you feel?" he said flatly. OK. Now I was pissing him off. He obviously wanted this to be dealt with so life could carry on as normal.

"Look…It's one of those things. We're both adults. We had too much to drink and…blah…you know," I replied matter of factly.

"Is that all?"

"What do you mean?" Sometimes I just wished people would be more direct.

"Did you enjoy yourself?"

"What?" Oh God...*really*? "Yes Colin. I enjoyed myself. Did you?" Shit. What if he said no and I'd just said yes?

"More than I imagined and I have a good imagination." He gave me a wicked grin and I burst out laughing.

"Right. Well, that's great then." I was crap at this kind of conversation.

He sat there, just looking at me, all steady and confident and allowing the silence to go on too long for my liking. I didn't know what to do so I started singing a Taylor Swift song in my head.

"Soph...I'd like to make more of this, if you'd like to?"

More of it? More of it how? Like booty calls or what? What did he mean? "As in...well... like, *last night kinda thing*?" I asked.

Colin started laughing. "Well ...yeah...that kinda thing *definitely* but more than that."

Too many thoughts, as usual, whirred in my head. Could I? Did I want to? He was gorgeous...it was fun... but...Colin was a free spirit and bored easily. It could ruin the friendship let alone the working relationship I'd need to maintain. I had kids and he didn't. I had a Brendon. That was enough to tip anyone over the edge. I came with more baggage than a 747. But that didn't matter right now... I didn't have money for fancy nights out anymore...I mean.. I couldn't expect him to pay for everything. No way. How could it work?

"Is that a no then?" he asked quietly, breaking my mind fill.

"No, no, no. Yes. No..." I stumbled.

"Which one Soph?" He looked deep into my eyes and I felt that pull from last night. Shit.

"I'd like to throw caution to the wind and say yes. But, I'm not sure Colin. I don't want to become one of your 'Trudies' and I don't want to ruin our current relationship." I looked at him directly and was proud of myself for being together and succinct.

"Well I'm going to take that as a yes Soph…and you don't even fall into the 'Trudie' bracket. Your qualities are unquantifiable." He winked at me.

I sat there, just looking at him.

"So, let's get down to it then," he said.

"Down to it? Here? …" I looked at him gone out.

"To work?" he offered.

Oh God, I thought. Of course. Yes, to work. Ugh. I felt like such a muppet. I stood up to leave.

"I'll speak to you later babe." He looked up with his big blue eyes.

Those eyes were going to kill me.

"Ok then," I said, and left his office like I'd just eaten a pile of hash brownies.

CHAPTER 22

I t was my final day at work and I felt somewhat depressed. The end of an era and a doorway to a different adventure. A new beginning that would hopefully see my son get through to the end of school with decent qualifications to support his brilliant mind and get him on the his next journey, wherever that may be.

I had my first meeting at Hillfields School this morning with Janice Armitage before I went to the office. I got ready slowly, savouring the moment and applying more effort than usual to my make up and attire. Tomorrow I'd be would be working from home after my school visit and would be able to dress how I pleased. Hmm, maybe I could go all boho hippy or something and invent a new me for my new role…Nah, maybe not.

I made pancakes for the kids which was probably a mistake as I didn't want them getting used to the idea. I left them in a warm oven whilst I opened the pile of letters on the side of the kitchen counter. Bills, more bills, an invite to neighbourhood watch and then a complete and utter shock. The large letter was addressed in floaty style, italic font and gilt edged. Maybe I'd won something? I opened it up and began to read:

To Sophie Rhodes,

Receipt for booking of Heavenly Spa Indulgence at Eden Hall.

Set within acres of luscious lawns this beautiful listed mansion, built in 1875 will be your sanctuary for the day. Whether you want to refresh and revive or unwind and relax, the first class facilities make sure all of your needs are met.

Whatever your pampering needs, escape to Eden hall for the perfect, peaceful getaway.

Includes 3 course meal at our beautiful restaurant and:

The relaxation day plus the Thalgo Indoceane Comforting Wrap. This is the ultimate therapy for those looking to pamper their skin. Enjoy soothing warm oils and light massage to the back and scalp followed by the application of a hydrating cream. Enveloped; drift away whilst these luxurious products hydrate and nourish the skin.

Paid in full: £161.00

What? I hadn't bought that! I turned the letter over to see if they'd made a mistake or who it was from but there was nothing. Just the letter, a booklet that made me want to head for Zen land right this second and a number for me to call to book my preferred day. Who the hell was this from? I put the letter in my bag so I could deal with it when I got to work.

We got to school and I parked up outside whilst Bryony and Brendon went in together. I made my way to reception to get my visitors pass.

"Hi" I said to the receptionist, "I'm going to be here pretty much every day for the next few weeks so can I just have a month's pass or something?"

"No, sorry, It's against our rules and regulations. You need to sign in and out every time...Is it for Mrs. Armitage?"

"No," I replied.

"Oh...?"

"Just kidding! Yes. For Mrs. Armitage. As usual." These people had no concept of playfulness.

Janice came down to collect me and we went upstairs to BASE. Brendon was already there removing all the white board pens.

"What are you doing?" I asked.

"Stopping that freak boy from winding me up."

I looked at Janice, puzzled.

"Yesterday, there was a pupil in here who was drawing on the white board. It's what he likes to do. However, the pen was making a squeaking noise and Brendon didn't like it. He told him to stop but the boy refused so Brendon snatched it out of his hand, removed all other pens and forced the boy to leave. Obviously it's gone down as an incident," she said.

"Brendon! That's nasty. It's not up to you what other people do. Put those pens back now!" I scolded.

"No. The noise does my head in. Not happening again."

"Brendon," Janice pressed, "I've made sure he won't be in here when you are. Plus now your timetable is cut down, it won't be a problem. Put down the pens and sit down so we can go through your lesson plan now it's been set. "

We all sat down, Brendon still holding tight to the fat markers. We went through the timetable and Brendon and I were made a copy.

"He's doing well in most subjects," Janice said, going through the reports, "though coursework needs updating. He can use some free time at The BASE to do that or at home. He is being put straight in for AS level for Ethics and philosophy because he's extremely good at it."

I was surprised by that. I couldn't picture Brendon as a philosopher. Maybe a professional hacker or a politician but a philosopher?"

"Why do you like that so much?" I asked him.

"Because you can argue and debate and change people's opinions. There's one girl in there that I hate though. She's as thick as fuck and needs to be removed."

"Don't be so rude and arrogant!" I wished he'd be more tolerant of people but I could never see it happening.

"It's true. She's stupid. I think my teacher even agrees. He's cool." It was rare I heard Brendon call a teacher cool.

"It's the only lesson he's never received a negative comment in, only positives." Janice pulled a mock astonished face.

Brendon was excused to go to his class and he put the

pens in a cupboard, high up, that only he could reach before leaving.

"Don't worry, we've got ladders." Janice said to me after he'd left, "sometimes it's just not worth the argument."

The reality of the situation ahead of me started to settle and I slumped a little in the plastic, blue chair. "I need to make this work Janice. I've left my job for this and I want him to get his qualifications."

"We can do it. If we stick together then we should get him through. To be honest he has been relatively good lately, aside from the controlling and vigilante type behaviour, he hasn't been *that* rude. I think that being on governors report has actually made him think. Not that he'd *ever* tell us that but he does raise his concerns with me sometimes."

I was glad that he did. Maybe things did seep through after all. I arranged to see Janice the following day and so forth and left the school feeling quite positive. However, I wasn't going to hold my breath. I'd been on these momentary highs before only to have them slashed ten minutes later when he'd got excluded for the day. This was going to be a continuous battle of highs and lows but a battle I was now ready for.

I arrived at work to find my desk covered in presents. I wanted to cry. Everyone gathered round whilst I opened them all up. I got a Starbucks card with £50 on so I could afford the odd luxury coffee when in town, three bottles of Rioja, a cinema ticket for the year so I could go out and watch films whenever I wanted, chocolates, a big mud pie from The Cheesecake Shop that Monica was already cutting into and a beautiful, silver bracelet with a four leafed clover charm, from Argento. When I opened my card I actually did start to shed a quiet tear as the messages were so touching.

> *'I've never felt so upset about losing something but I want only the best for you Soph. You'd better come in EVERY week. Johnno XX'*

And then there was Colin's.

> *'You may be walking out of this office but I won't let you walk out of our lives.' Colin X'*

Where was Colin? I'd got so caught up with the immediate gathering that I'd only just noticed he wasn't there. "Where's Colin?" I asked the group.

"He got called into a big meeting. He'll be out most of the day." Monica replied.

I was devastated. He wasn't here for my last day at work. Plus we hadn't spoken since the 'about last night' speech and now I felt awkward and vulnerable. Maybe he'd had a change of heart.

I sat tucking into my slice of mud pie as I packaged all my goodies away and set to actually doing some work. Suddenly my phone rang. It was Rhodes, Karl Rhodes.

"Hello." I greeted him.

"Hi," he replied without any emotion, "where on earth were you the other evening?"

"What? Oh, you mean when I went to the World Service?"

"I don't know where you went except that you were with your boss. I had a phone call from Brendon at midnight wondering what to do and whether he should ring you. It woke me up. "

"Oh. Sorry." I couldn't believe Brendon had called his Dad! Little snitch bag. He'd kept that one quiet.

"Why were you out so late? Is anything even open past midnight? It's a little late to be leaving the kids on their own."

"I'm never usually that late home if I get to go out, so don't pull that one. It was a special event so it went on longer than usual." Trust him to spoil my happy mood, "plus the kids are fine, the house is secure, they have my number, friends' numbers and neighbours. What do you want me to do? Never go out anywhere?"

"That's not what I said. I think it's a little late to be out with your boss and you need to be aware of your responsibilities."

Wanker.

"A little late to be out with my boss? I wonder if Sarah's mum says that to her," I said sarcastically.

"There's no need to be facetious. I was ringing to make sure there wasn't a problem."

"Did you receive my spreadsheet?" I asked, changing the subject before I lost my temper.

"Yes. I've made some corrections and alterations which we need to go through. I'll call in to see you this weekend."

Of course he had.

"Well make sure you call first in case I'm out. Now, I must go as it's my last day at work and I'm busy with my colleagues."

"Right. I'll see you later." He hung up. I looked at my phone and thought about deleting him.

The day flew by faster than any other, probably because I didn't want it to and though it had been nice it was tinged with sadness. By 4pm I sat at my desk with a cuppa and ate yet another chocolate from the pile on my desk.

"No more Soph!" Johnno exclaimed, "they're bad for you and you won't eat your dinner!"

"You can't buy me something and then tell me it's bad for me! Besides, I probably won't eat dinner."

"Yes you will."

"OK, Dad."

My phone beeped:

MSG From: COLIN FRAY: I can't stop thinking about you.

My heart did a happy dance and a smile spread across my face. I re read the message several times before responding.

SOPHIE RHODES: Don't worry, you'll get over that in a few weeks.

COLIN FRAY: I doubt that. Sorry I missed your big day. Meeting.

SOPHIE RHODES: It's OK. That's life. Thanks for all the presents.

COLIN FRAY: I didn't want to see you walk out anyway so maybe it's a blessing.

I left the office at the end of the day having been hugged to death, kissed a hundred times and with a whole load of promises to keep. My new waterproof mascara that had been given to me from the beauty department, had leaked down my face leaving me looking like Gene Simmons in a rain storm.

When I arrived back at the ranch, Bryony was sat at the kitchen table doing her art homework and listening to music. I spent some time helping her paint even though she kept telling me I was doing it wrong. Painting by numbers was probably more up my street but it helped me ignore the feeling of loss that enveloped me.

"Where's Brendon?" I asked.

"He's at Jessies. I think he's gone there for tea."

I made her some cheese on toast as she painted flowers in a Georgia O' Keeffe style and I marvelled at her talent. I couldn't eat anything as I had seriously overdosed on chocolate. I decided, instead, to open one of the bottles of Rioja I had received and have a glass of that to celebrate and commiserate and sat next to Bryony as the red and pink hues of the oil paint married themselves together.

A while later Brendon arrived. He looked *very* happy and chilled. I sniffed the air for traces of drugs.

"Hey *Mommy*." He gave me a big hug, "did you get my present?

"What present?" I looked around the room for signs of gifts.

"It should have come in the post. They emailed me to say it had… It's a spa day. You like those don't you?"

Oh my God. The letter. I'd completely forgotten about it.

"You? You bought me that? Are you *serious*?" I was in shock.

"Yes. To say thank you for everything you do. I know I make life hard for you."

I clasped my hand to my heart before it broke in two. "You can't afford that. How did you pay for it? You shouldn't have…really. Thank you so much. You're my sweetheart!"

"I saved up all my birthday money."

"What?" I hugged him hard and vowed in my heart to pay him back, "But that money is for you to spend on yourself…not for anyone else."

"Don't you like it then?" He stiffened and pulled away from me.

"Yes of *course* I do! I LOVE spa days and it's just what I needed, " I sighed, "I'm not being ungrateful, I just don't want you spending that kind of money on me...but thank you. Thank you *so* much." His generosity had always dumbfounded me. Like everything he did, it was extreme. I changed the subject before I offended him.

"You seem very happy and relaxed. You haven't been smoking weed have you?" I teased.

"No. But I just got a blow job from a Catholic girl. Result!" He high fived his sister who burst out laughing.

I gripped the side of the kitchen counter to steady myself.

"I beg your pardon." I looked at him. "I can't believe you've done that."

"I didn't do anything Mum! She did it all on her own."

"And YOU," I turned to Bryony, "shouldn't even know what that means never mind giving him a high five!"

"OMG Mum, we're not five years old!"

"Was it good?" Bryony continued like I wasn't there.

"What! OH MY GOD, go to your room!" I shouted at her, snatching the paintbrush from her hand.

"Well Bry, it's like a pizza," Brendon replied, "even if it's a bad pizza, it's *still* a pizza!"

"I hear ya bro!" Bryony laughed as she collected her art book and left the kitchen.

"You're outrageous." I said to Brendon as I stormed upstairs to my bedroom.

SOPHIE'S THROUGHWAY

I lay on my bed and tried to remember what it was like to be fifteen to sixteen years old before I went into psychopathic parent. I needed to calm myself down a bit.

I clicked on my word game and located 'The Voice'. He was now listed in the 'Game Over' category of my virtual board. Due to lack of play the game had automatically resigned. I felt like I'd lost my first cyber love. I'd never get to know who that mystery Californian was who'd won my heart with his words.

My phone rang as I stared at the lost game from across the pond. It was Colin. I could hear the noise of a car in the background.

"Soph… get ready I'm on my way to fetch you."

"What? Why? Fetch me for what?" ARRR, I wasn't ready to go anywhere.

"Your leaving do. Johnno's arranged it as a surprise, you can't let him down. Or me for that matter!"

"Aww that's so sweet…that's why he tried to stop me eating all those chocolates. I don't think I'll be able to eat anything…And I'm not prepared!" I panicked.

"Just get your shoes on, I'll be there in ten. It's nothing glam, just a few drinks and a pizza."

I lay back on my pillow and laughed my head off.

"What's so funny?" said Colin, laughing along at my outburst.

"Ah, nothing. I'm looking forward to it. After all, there's no such thing as a bad pizza, right?"